A Cord of Three Strands

A Cord of Three Strands

Holly Moulder

White Pelican Press

ISBN 13: 978-0-9790405-1-1
10: 0-9790405-1-5
LOC 2007941750
Book production: Tabby House
Cover design and map: Carol Tornatore

White Pelican Press
132 Marcella Avenue
Sharpsburg, GA 30277

Dedication

In memory of Gordon Craig,
who loved his grandson Donald very well indeed,
and
in memory of Stanley William Fisher and Frank Johnson Barndt,
who, through the love of their children,
touched the life of their granddaughter Holly
in many wonderful ways.

Contents

(handwritten: goal to read)

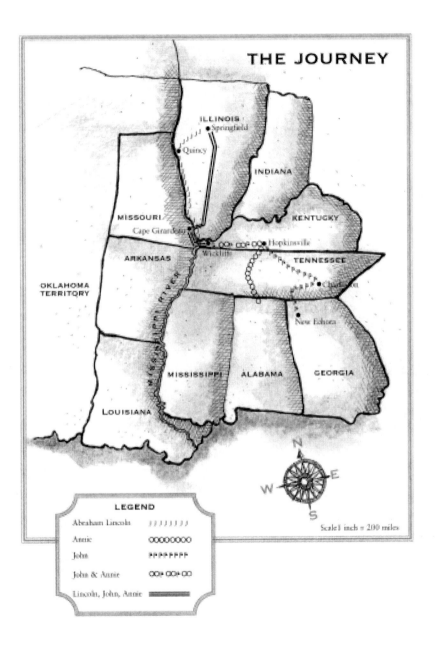

THE JOURNEY

ILLINOIS
● Springfield
● Quincy

INDIANA

MISSOURI
Cape Girardeau ●

KENTUCKY

● Hopkinsville

Wickliffe

ARKANSAS

TENNESSEE

OKLAHOMA
TERRITORY

● Chattanooga

MISSISSIPPI RIVER

● New Echota

MISSISSIPPI   ALABAMA   GEORGIA

LOUISIANA

N
W   E
S

Scale 1 inch = 200 miles

LEGEND

Abraham Lincoln	,,,,,,,,
Annie	OOOOOOOO
John	PPPPPPPP
John & Annie	OOP OOP OO
Lincoln, John, Annie	▬▬▬▬▬

9

1
Atsila

Neither the old man nor the boy noticed the inky spiral of smoke snaking its way into the cerulean sky. Both were intent upon their work, carefully selecting plants and herbs to use as medicine for The People. They had wandered farther than usual from their cabin in search of willow root, for Gray Hawk insisted on just the right texture, age and color. John had learned at an early age that only the best ingredients were ever to be used in his grandfather's salves and potions.

"But, Grandfather," John had protested when they began the long day of hunting and digging. "The other boys will be playing ball on the field in the village, and I want to watch. Must this be done today?"

"Yes, Grandson, today it must be done. The other boys are not of the Blue Clan as you are, and their grandfather is not the shaman. They are not responsible for the health of The People as we are." He spoke firmly to the boy, but the twinkle in his dark eyes and the smile teasing the corners of his creased mouth reassured his grandson that there still might be time for play today. young

Resignedly, John had collected his gathering sack and knives, and prepared himself for a long morning trek in the woods. He tucked his river cane flute into his belt, for he never went anywhere without it. His father had carved it for him, and had begun teaching him how to play. It was a great honor to make music with the men of the village, and John already played as well as some of the men twice his age. He practiced constantly.

His grandfather, known to The People as Gray Hawk, was a respected elder of the Cherokee tribe. He was the great healer of the village, and was teaching his grandson the secrets of medicine, which The People called Nun-wa-ti. Sometimes, however, he tried to teach John more than a thirteen-year-old boy wanted to know. Today, Grandfather had rejected plant after plant, showing John the faults of each until he finally found one that was perfect. He followed the ancient teachings of The People, taking only the third plant that he found. The others must be left for future use. The search had taken them far from their home, and only now did John notice the dark column of smoke marring the azure sky.

"Grandfather, what is burning? Look! *Atsila!* Fire!" Ominous black clouds had gathered over the place where the village stood. John stopped his digging, dropped his tool, and limped as quickly as he could toward a clearing in the trees to get a better look.

"Come, Grandson," the old man said, eyeing the darkening horizon. Although his hair was silvered with age and the maple-colored skin of his face was deeply lined, his vision was as sharp as his grandson's. "We must hurry. The People are in trouble."

Old man and boy trudged through the forest underbrush as fast as their frail bodies would allow. Grandfather, stricken with the pain and stiffness of aging bones, leaned heavily on his walking stick for support. John moved almost as slowly on his crippled leg, an accident of his birth. His right foot was twisted, turned inward, and his knee had been weakened by the strain. His leg caused John constant pain, but neither grandfather nor grandson thought of pain now. They thought only of their people as they struggled and stumbled through the woods toward their home.

Staring down from the hill that overlooked the town, John beheld a horror that drove knives of fear straight into his heart. The town was burning! Every building was ablaze. In the streets, sobbing women watched their homes disappear as raging fire demolished wooden roofs and porches. Screaming children clenched their mother's skirts. Men darted in and out of burning houses, braving flames and their own fear in order to save some household possessions. Very little was left to save. Blue-uniformed soldiers on horseback rode from house to house, flaming torches in hand, setting fire to the small wooden structures that The People had called their homes.

"Grandfather, look at our house!" John exclaimed. Without hesitation, he clumsily scrambled down the steep slope, scuttling and sliding in the rocks until, covered with bloody scratches and red dirt, he reached the bottom. Shoving his way through the crowds of hysterical people, John arrived at the cabin he had shared with his grandfather for all of his thirteen years. Black smoke poured through its windows. Brilliant amber flames lashed viciously at the front steps and the wooden plank porch. Still, John pushed at the heavy door, hoping to salvage some of his grandfather's possessions. The irreplaceable bowls and vials, the mortar and pestle, all would be destroyed. They had been used by generations of healers before Gray Hawk, and John knew that one day they would belong to him. He could not let the flames destroy them!

As he rammed his way through the thick plank door, John realized he was too late. Thick smoke streamed through the opening, burning his eyes. Heat from the flames coursed over him, threatening to ignite his very skin. If he went any farther, he knew he would perish.

Backing away from the inferno, John turned to see his grandfather standing in the front yard, beckoning to him. Making his way down the charred remains of their front steps, John hung his head in shame and grief. His long black hair, filled with smoke and ash, hung like a filthy curtain across his face. He could not allow himself to look into the eyes of his grandfather. He could not bear to see the disappointment that must surely be reflected there. He had failed his grandfather.

"Come, my grandson. There is nothing more for us here,"

Grandfather said, as he lifted John's face to meet his own. Gray Hawk's eyes were heavy with tears, whether from smoke or from sorrow John was not certain. "We had been told that this might happen, but we chose to ignore the warnings. And now, the white men have come to take our land and our home. Their greed has driven them to this. The soldiers have ordered us into their wagons, and we have nothing to take with us but the clothing we wear."

The old man laid his arm around John's shoulders, and walked unsteadily toward the lines of men, women, and children who were being loaded onto the wagons by impatient soldiers. "John, hold your head high. They strip us of our possessions, but not our dignity." Suddenly the boy stopped and turned to stare up into his grandfather's saddened face.

"But what of Grandmother, and my mother, and my father?" John pleaded. "Who will care for their graves when we are gone? The white soldiers will not respect the resting places of our dead!" Now tears streamed down John's cheeks, and he did not try to hide them.

Gray Hawk answered gently, "Grandson, we will leave them here, in the hands of our god. The Great Spirit will care for those of The People who must be left behind. I am thankful to the Great Spirit that your grandmother is not alive to witness this terrible day."

Never before had John heard his grandfather speak with such pain and grief. This day of sorrow would surely live in his heart forever.

2
Tadeyastatakuhl

Clusters of dirty, distraught Indians watched helplessly as the soldiers hoisted Gray Hawk roughly onto the back of the wagon with the other elders of their village. John limped along the road beside his grandfather as the slow-moving wagon took its place in line with others. Clouds of smoke swirled over the town, clinging to the trees and shrubs like thick, spidery webs. A clay-colored haze enveloped The People and soldiers alike, searing their eyes and burning dry throats. Tired horses tread wearily along in the dust, pulling their woeful load of weeping people, the remnants of a proud Cherokee village.

"Look, Grandfather," John said as he pointed toward a two-story wooden house, painted white with green shutters on the windows. The soldiers had spared this house from the inferno that had swept through the village. Its owners, Charles and Susannah Thompson, were white missionaries and teachers who had come to share their Christian faith with the Cherokee people whom they had grown to love. On their porch, the Thompsons stood weeping, arms wrapped around each other, watching as the soldiers herded The People from their ruined homes and onto the wagons.

"Please may I go speak with them, Grandfather? May I tell them good-bye?" John pleaded. A bored-looking soldier, accompanying the wagon on horseback, overheard John's questions, and shrugged his shoulders. The boy interpreted the gesture as consent.

15

"Go quickly," Gray Hawk said. "Tell them farewell, for I believe we will not see this place again. Give them my thanks for all that they have taught you. Give them this as well." Grandfather took an eagle feather from a leather cord he wore around his neck. "Tell them to keep this always, and to remember that the Great Spirit watches over His people. He will care for us, and for them."

Not so long ago, Gray Hawk had regarded the Thompsons as enemies of The People. They had brought change with them, a change that had affected the entire village. Mr. Thompson had preached to The People about a new god, one that was different from the ancient Spirit that had guided the Cherokee for generations, and many of the villagers had come to accept this new religion, rejecting the old ways. Gray Hawk had been angered by this.

But the Thompsons had also brought books with them to educate the young people of the tribe. Every day, John had attended classes taught by Mrs. Thompson, and he had learned to read the writings of the white man. Now Gray Hawk's grandson could read both the words of the white man, and the writings of Sequoyah, creator of the Cherokee alphabet. When he was eight years old, John had read aloud to his grandfather each edition of the *Cherokee Phoenix*, The People's newspaper. In this way, Gray Hawk and John had kept abreast of the war of words that was occurring between The People and the United States government until the spring of 1834, when the government forced the newspaper to stop printing. Gray Hawk was grateful to the Thompsons for the opportunity they had afforded his grandson by teaching him to read.

Over the years, both Charles and Susannah had won the respect of the villagers through their obvious love for the Cherokee children. On this day of sorrow, the missionaries wept for their adopted people, and watched helplessly as the Cherokee were led away to a strange land to the west.

John hobbled across the wide lawn to his teachers and wrapped his arms around them, holding them close. He felt their tears mingle with his own as they whispered their good-byes.

"Thank you for all that you have done for us," John stammered through his tears. "I will not forget your lessons or your kindness. My grandfather sends this to you, in gratitude, for teaching me." John pressed the feather into Charles' palm, and looked deeply into his sad eyes. "He asks that you keep it with you always, to help you remember The People." Choked with emotion, Charles could only nod silently.

"Thank Gray Hawk for us," Miss Susannah murmured. Grief clawed at her throat, making it difficult for her to speak. "We will not forget your people, or you," she whispered. "Our prayers go with you."

Several of the soldiers yelled angrily at John, and motioned for him to get in the wagon. After one last hug for his friends, he shuffled down the porch steps and across the yard. Awkwardly he climbed up in the wagon and sat down next to his grandfather. Leaning over the side, John called to the Thompsons. "*Tadeyastatakuhl!*" he cried first in Cherokee, and then translating his message into English, he called out, "We will see each other again!" As the wagon jerked forward, John watched the scorched remains of the village slowly disappear, until nothing remained but a black smudge floating across the cobalt blue of a Cherokee sky.

* * *

The sun had nearly disappeared from the horizon when the soldiers halted the sad procession of wagons at the gate of a hastily constructed fort. A palisade of tall logs served as the walls that surrounded a large, open space in the center. Smoke from the burning village still hung in the air over the camp, a harsh reminder of the day's horror.

"Get out," one soldier shouted gruffly, as he yanked on Gray Hawk's arm to pull him from the wagon. The old man stumbled, but grabbed hold of one of the wagon's wooden planks, and was able to steady himself. Gray Hawk angrily glared at the soldier named Corporal Tidwell, this man who treated The People with such disrespect. Tidwell, short of both stature and temper, had sharp blue eyes that were cold and hard, and a thin face that was creased with dirt. His uniform smelled of sweat, and his light brown hair, curled beneath a battered cap, smelled of smoke. The scent of whiskey, sickly sweet, clung to him like a shroud. His words were callous and laced with venom, and his rough actions were designed to hurt the children and the aged. He sneered at the suffering he caused.

As he and his grandfather joined the line of Indians filing through the gate, John could see that there was only one small building in the fort, a tiny cabin in the corner. More soldiers were standing in front of it, smoking and laughing. Glancing around, John saw that some of The People had already begun to make sleeping places for themselves by laying blankets and robes on the cold, damp soil. Small fires appeared as darkness closed in. Soldiers went from group to group, distributing bacon and cornmeal for the evening meal. John and Gray Hawk shared a meager supper with some of their neighbors, but no one was very hungry, and everyone ate in silence. Grief filled the camp, and despair covered The People like a wet, heavy robe.

It was Gray Hawk who finally spoke. He rose to his feet, and stood tall. His voice sounded surprisingly strong, like a young man's, and everyone gathered to hear the words of the elder, the man they loved and respected. He spoke in the language of his captors, for he wanted them to understand his words.

"Come, children, and sit before me. Listen, young and old, to a story of our people. Find comfort and strength in the tradition of our words.

"In the beginning, no fire existed on the Earth. Can you imagine how cold and dark a place this must have been? But then, the Thunders sent their lightning to a hollow sycamore that grew on an island, and a fire began.

"The animals all knew that the fire was there on the island because they could see the smoke, but the island was surrounded by water, and no one could get to it. They held a meeting to decide what to do. Every creature that could swim or fly wanted to be the one to go gather the fire. Raven, being strong and swift, was chosen to be the first to try.

main point in story

"Raven flew to the island, and landed in the branches of the sycamore tree. But before he could decide what to do, the heat from the fire singed his feathers black, and he flew back, frightened.

"Next, Screech Owl asked to go. He, too, flew across the water and perched in the limbs of the tree. A cloud of hot air burned Screech Owl's eyes, and he struggled to find his way home. He survived, but his eyes remain red to this very day. Others tried to capture the fire, but none of the birds or the snakes succeeded."

Although the children had heard this familiar story many times, they listened intently as grandfather continued. Even the adults were charmed by the beauty of the story and the expression with which it was being told.

Grandfather continued, "Finally, tiny Water Spider volunteered to go. She had soft black hair and red stripes on her body. She could easily go anywhere she chose, but how could one so small succeed where animals bigger and stronger had failed?

"The others asked her how she would carry the fire. And she simply replied, 'Watch me!' And they did!

"She spun a thread and wove it into a bowl. She put the bowl on her back, and then she ran across the water to the island. She climbed down the hollow trunk of the sycamore tree to the fire and placed one little coal of fire into her bowl. She walked carefully back across the water to where all the creatures waited for her. They cheered her for her intelligence and bravery. And since that time, we have had fire.

"I tell this story now because I want you to remember how the Great Spirit has always taken care of us, His creation. Using the weakest of us, He completes His greatest works. We should not fear what this government or these soldiers can do to us. The Great

story of fire

Spirit cares for us. His strong arms will guide us on this journey, and He will protect the Principal People, just as He always has."

With those words, Grandfather sat down. Grunting their agreement, the other elders and the principal women of the village joined him. Several of the men gathered to play the traditional instruments that produced the eerily beautiful music which brought The People great comfort. John smiled wearily. *Even in the midst of today's horror,* he thought, *the men know that their music might be the only way to bring comfort to The People.*

The other women and the children sang little songs as they prepared for sleep, their faces shining with hope. The blanket of misery that had covered the camp rolled back into the night.

Corporal Tidwell made his way toward John. "Who is that old man anyway? Why do they listen to him? Don't you know where you're going? Some stupid story about a spider isn't going to save you from what's coming. He's just wasting his breath."

"That man is my *enisi*, my grandfather," John replied proudly. "He is a great teacher and the people respect him. You would do well to listen to him."

Tidwell spat on the ground in disgust, and stalked away, mumbling to himself. As he watched the man stride toward the group of soldiers guarding the gate, John couldn't help but wonder what the future would hold for The People. Could the Great Spirit truly care for The People by using the smallest and weakest of us?

Confident in the words that his grandfather had spoken, John took his flute from his belt and went to join the other musicians.

3
The Trumpet Sounds

A big ball o' butter, rollin' across a sorghum sky, Annie thought as she studied the bright moon shining in the dark Alabama night. She was curled up on the front stoop of the slave cabin, her back resting against the wood planks. She pulled her worn shawl tightly around her thin shoulders, stretching it so that the meager fabric could cover her bare feet. The first fall chill was in the air, and Annie was grateful. She loved the cool mornings and evenings much better than the heavy heat of Alabama summers. Still, Annie found it hard to enjoy the cool evening breezes when her empty belly was grumbling. "Bet the master eats all he wants of butter and sorghum and molasses and biscuits and any other fine food he has a craving for!" Pangs of hunger reminded her that the Mistress Ellidge had denied her a supper tonight. But food wasn't all that she hungered for.

"It was just a biscuit," she brooded aloud. It didn't matter to her that no one heard, except for the occasional night bird passing by on its evening rounds. "Li'l Jacob was so hungry and he wouldn't stop crying. Miss Becca was just gonna throw the rest of them out. The master's family didn't want no more. Why couldn't Jacob have just one?" Her calloused hand made a fist and struck the rough-hewn wall. She winced. The unfairness of some people having so much, while others had barely enough to survive, angered twelve-year-old Annie. "He's just a baby," she said aloud, rubbing her sore hand. Standing up and stretching her long, thin body, Annie walked into the cabin.

The faint glow of a single lantern barely illuminated the hut where Annie lived with her mama, papa, fifteen-year-old brother Isaiah, and tiny Jacob. A small fire on the hearth gave little light and even less warmth to the tiny room. In a shadow in the corner, Jacob was already tucked in his pallet, sleeping soundly, quiet at last. Close to the lantern, Mama hummed softly as she peered at the shirt she was trying to mend, her weak eyes failing in the dim light.

"My Lord calls me, he calls me by the thunder, the trumpet sounds it in my soul, I ain't got long to stay here," she sang sweetly.

Sighing softly, she put her needle down, and laid her head against the high back of the rocking chair. "Just restin' my eyes," she would always tell Annie.

Papa and Isaiah sat close to the fire. With their heads together, deep in secret conversation, they looked identical, as if one had been made of the same bone and sinew as the other. They were talking tonight about something important, Annie knew, because they sat closely together, knees and shoulders touching, their words wrapping around them like a heavy cloak.

As Annie gathered the threadbare quilt of her bed close to her, stomach pains reminded her once again of the events of the day, and the reason for her hunger tonight. Earlier that afternoon, Annie had been working in the kitchen, helping Miss Becca, the cook, prepare the evening meal that was to be served in the main house. All day, little Jacob had been following Annie around as usual, "helping" in his two-year-old way. In truth, Jacob had spent most of his toddler life traipsing after Annie like a little chestnut-colored puppy looking for scraps to eat and people to love. Fortunately, he had always found the love he needed. Since his birth he had been showered with warm affection by the slaves who labored on Herbert Ellidge's plantation, but scraps of food had always been scarce. So today, as on many days, Jacob had been hungry and whiny.

"Annie, Annie, Annie," he whimpered, rubbing his little belly. "I hungry, hungry, hungry!" Big tears dripped down his face, washing away the dusty Alabama clay from his cheeks, and melting his sister's heart.

Annie picked him up and tried to console him. "Jacob, be a good boy now, and when I finish sweepin' up here in the kitchen, we'll go look at the brand-new calf in the master's barn. There now, won't that be fun?"

But Jacob would not be comforted, and he continued to cry. Desperately, Annie searched around the kitchen for something to satisfy the hungry child. On the kitchen counter, a plate of biscuits left over from the morning's bountiful breakfast peeked out from beneath a red gingham napkin. "Just one," Annie whispered to Jacob as she whisked a doughy treat out from under the cloth. The little boy eagerly grabbed the biscuit in both hands and stuffed huge chunks in his mouth. His face and hands were covered with crumbs, evidence of his crime, when Mistress Ellidge unexpectedly entered the room.

"What is this child eating? Who gave him permission to do so?" Mistress Ellidge was livid. Her puffy cheeks had turned bright red, and her tiny brown eyes were hard and cold. The rolls of her heavy body shook with rage as her fat fingers snatched the remains of Jacob's treat out of the toddler's tiny hands. "Did you give him this?" she demanded, glaring at Annie. Frightened, Jacob whimpered.

"Yes, ma'am, I did," Annie began quietly, hesitatingly. "I thought that the biscuits were just leftovers from the breakfast this morning, and I didn't think anyone would be wantin' any more so . . ."

Smack! Mistress Ellidge's fleshy palm struck Annie's soft cheek, nearly knocking both her and Jacob to the ground. Instead, Annie fell heavily against the old kitchen work table, sending a large bowl of flour and a pitcher of fresh milk crashing to the floor. "Look what you've done!" screamed the mistress. "Clean up the mess you've made!" Struggling to her feet, Annie set Jacob down in a corner and quickly grabbed a cleaning cloth. On her knees in the mess, Annie began to scrub. Glancing up at the angry woman, it seemed to Annie that Mistress Ellidge's face was now impossibly red, a huge crimson boil ready to burst. "And for your punishment," the mistress screeched, "you'll have no supper tonight! Perhaps your hunger will help remind you not to steal food from the mouths of your master's family!"

Then, leaning down as far as her rotund body would allow, Mistress Ellidge ended her tirade with a threat spat in Annie face. Glowering at the frightened slave, the woman hissed, "If I catch you stealing from this kitchen again, you'll be missing more than your supper. Next time, girl, you'll be missing some skin off your back, peeled away by the overseer's whip." Straightening, she lifted her fancy skirts so as not to soil them in the floury paste. Mistress Ellidge then regally strode from the room, leaving a hungry Jacob and an angry Annie in her wake. But before she crossed the threshold into the yard, the mistress picked up the plate of biscuits from the table and dumped them into the bucket of garbage by the door. "I suppose these will do for the pigs," she smirked. Annie kept her eyes on the floor, her anger boiling at the cruelty of her mistress. "Someday . . . ," was all she could utter through her clenched teeth.

Tonight Annie had to stay late in the kitchen, and when she had finally gotten back to the cabin, the small supper Mama had prepared was already gone. Papa, Isaiah, and Jacob had devoured everything, leaving little more than a few crumbs of corn bread. Annie always ate her meals in the kitchen with Miss Becca, so her mother never bothered to save food for her. Besides, the two grown men and one growing boy quickly consumed any food Mama could scrounge up. So, Annie had only her anger to fill her stomach..

Now as she tossed and turned on her pallet waiting for sleep to come, she listened to the soft murmurings of Papa and Isaiah. She strained to hear the whispered words being spoken between the two men.

"Isaiah," Papa whispered, "I know Master Ellidge plans to sell me and you to the Boardmans, that big place on the other side of town. The crop's been poor this year, and we're two, good, hard-working men. Selling us could help him pay off his debts in town, and he'd never miss us. Michael's the one been telling me this. He heard the master talking it all over with Mister Boardman." Michael was Master Ellidge's overseer. He was also, Annie knew, the biggest gossip on the whole plantation.

"We'll never see Mama or Annie or Jacob," Isaiah replied. "Who's going to look after them if we're gone so far away? They can't split up our family like this, can they, Papa? Would Master Ellidge do something so mean?"

Papa paused a moment. "He would if it meant taking care of his business. He doesn't care anything for his slaves or their families. He'd send us away for sure for a few dollars."

The dying fire in the grate shifted, sending a shower of sparks up the chimney. In the sudden burst of light, Annie could see her father's face clearly. He was angry, and his eyes flashed as he spoke. "We're going to leave here, son. You and me, Mama, Annie, and little Jacob are going to get away. I've heard of some of our people running north to live as free men, not slaves. I've heard talk in the fields that there are runaways out there who made it to freedom and then have come back to help others find their way. Tomorrow I'll see what more I can find out. I've got plans to make and people to talk to. Keep this to yourself, Isaiah. Master Ellidge would send both of us to the whipping post if he knew what we were planning. And don't say anything yet to your Mama or your brother or sister. We'll tell them when it's time."

Isaiah and Papa moved to their beds. Papa crawled under the blanket with Mama, and Isaiah covered himself with a quilt as he huddled in the corner beside Jacob.

Her empty stomach forgotten, Annie could barely keep from jumping off her pallet and dancing for joy. "Runaway!" she sang to herself. "Runaway! Runaway! I'm going be free!"

4

Lions

"We can leave Sunday morning," Papa told his family as they gathered around the small table in their cabin. The weather had stayed cool, and Annie shivered in the evening air despite the blanket wrapped around her shoulders. "We'll just act like we're going to Sunday meeting, and after the service we'll slip out the side door and hurry through the woods to the old mill road. A wagon will be waiting for us there."

Annie spoke up. "But, Papa, won't people notice us? Won't they see us leaving?" As excited as she was by the thought of getting away from Mistress Ellidge and the plantation, she knew that there would be terrible consequences if they were caught. She had seen one young man beaten nearly to death because he had tried to run away. Slave catchers hired by Master Ellidge had captured him and dragged him back to the plantation. The master himself had tied him to the whipping post, and had beaten him until the slave's bare back had been covered with bloody red stripes. Annie shivered at the thought of that happening to someone in her family.

Her father reached over and took her hand in his. He spoke to her gently. "Annie, there is a chance that our plan might be found out, but we just have to be careful. If we are to be together as a family, we're going to have to take the risk.

"We will not be able to carry anything with us. That could raise suspicion. We will take only the clothes on our backs, and

26

we will behave as if nothing is out of the ordinary. The man who has agreed to drive the wagon has told me that he will take us to people who will help us travel to a place in the North. Black folk are free there, and we will be safe."

Isaiah grinned at that, and snatched up Annie is his long arms. "We'll be free, girl!" he exclaimed. He swung her joyfully around the room, laughing in the fading light of the day. "No more sweeping a white man's kitchen floors! No more empty belly for Jacob! No more backbreaking days in the hot sun raising crops for someone else's family! We'll be able to do whatever *we* want!" Annie laughed with him, caught up in his arms and in the joy of the moment.

So excited and happy were they that no one in the cabin noticed the long shadow of a man on the stoop, someone who had been carefully listening to every word.

* * *

Will Sunday every get here? Annie wondered as she labored for the next several days under the watchful gaze of Miss Becca. Annie could barely keep her mind on her work, and so the cook had to correct her often for making mistakes or forgetting her chores.

"Annie, what are you daydreaming about? You haven't cleaned the kitchen properly in days, and you're falling behind in getting those dishes done. Keep your mind on the task at hand, girl. You don't want Mistress Ellidge to get hold of you again, do you?" Miss Becca was obviously exasperated.

"No, ma'am," Annie answered. "I'll do better." And with that, she set to work determinedly. She would scrub, shine and polish that kitchen until it glowed. And what would be her reward for all of this extra hard work? Why, freedom in that far away land to the north, of course!

* * *

Annie's days trickled by slower than molasses pouring from a jar. From sunrise to sunset she worked hard in the kitchen, at last earning praises from a relieved Miss Becca. Each night, the family huddled together in the little cabin, planning their new lives. Papa had determined that he would try to find employment as a blacksmith since he knew that work, and thought surely it would pay well in the North. Isaiah would work with him, learning the trade, until he was old enough to start out on his own. Mama would try to pick up small jobs as a seamstress so that she could work at home and take care of little Jacob. Everyone seemed to have a plan, except Annie.

"What about me?" Annie ventured one evening. "What will I do? I can clean kitchens or scrub floors. Would that help?" She earnestly desired to make some contribution to her family's well-being. Surely she could earn a little money to help buy food or to put towards warm clothing for her baby brother. Annie had heard that it could get very cold in the North during the winter, and it pained her to think of Jacob suffering.

Mama smiled broadly at Annie. "You'll have more important things to do than clean somebody else's house, child. We're going to find a teacher for you, Annie, someone who can show you how to read and write and work numbers. You've got the brains for it, for sure, and you'd be a great help to Papa and me."

The light sparkling then in Annie's eyes outshone the brightest star in the evening sky. "School!" she exclaimed. "School for me? Oh, Mama! Papa!" There were hugs all around, as Annie danced around the little table. Even Jacob gave a squeal of delight as his big sister squeezed him tight.

"I'll work hard. I promise! I'll be the best student those northern teachers have ever seen. You'll be so proud of me!"

* * *

At last Sunday arrived. Heavy gray clouds swept through the tall Alabama pines, bringing with them cold, miserable bursts of rain. Disheartened, Annie shivered as she peeked out the cabin door, only to have her face slapped by a brutal gust of winter wind.

"Mama, it's bitter cold out there. Poor Jacob will be frozen before we ever even get him to church!"

"Annie, don't you see?" Mama replied calmly. "This is a great blessing. We can wear every stitch of clothing we own under our jackets and no one will think anything about it. If it had been warm and sunny, we would have had to wear our summer shifts with no warm clothes to comfort us on our journey north! God has already started showing his provision for us!"

"Oh, Mama, you're right!" Annie remarked, delighted. "I'll start getting ready right now. I don't have much to take with me, but I'm thankful right now for each stitch of hand-me-down dresses I have!" Annie began layering on every garment she could find, from her torn woolen stockings to the moth-eaten sweater that was once owned by the master's daughter. When she finished dressing, she looked like a roly-poly twirling round and round on a poplar leaf in an autumn breeze.

"Mama, I'm going to pop!" she giggled as she sashayed around the room.

Mama smiled at her laughing daughter. "Hurry now and get Jacob ready," she said. "Papa and Isaiah will be back from their chores and it will be time for us to go. Wrap him as warmly as you can, Annie."

Mama, Annie, and Jacob were ready when Papa and Isaiah arrived back at the cabin. "I hid the blankets behind some bushes near the church," Papa said as the little family started to leave. "We'll carry them with us to the meeting place on the old mill road." Reaching behind Mama, he pulled the door of the tiny cabin shut with a resolute bang. "That's done," he said firmly, his breath making small, white puffs in the chilly air. "Now, let's go to church and pray for God's strength and protection as we begin this journey."

* * *

Run to Jesus, face the danger,
I don't expect to stay
Much longer here!
I thought I heard them say
There were lions on the way,
I don't expect to stay much longer here!

The little group of slaves huddling in the church sang the praise song with all the enthusiasm they could muster on this cold Sunday. No one seemed to notice that Annie sang a little louder this morning than she usually did. The words of the familiar hymn had special meaning for her today. She knew that this song was about going to be with Jesus, and that the lions they were singing about were the temptations that the devil used to lead people away from the path to heaven. But for Annie, the words meant something else altogether today. "I don't expect to stay much longer here!" she sang, smiling. *I'm really on my way,* she thought. *I am leaving here! And lions, you better look out because there is nothing that can get between me and my freedom!*

* * *

"I'm telling you, it's too dangerous!" the white-haired man exclaimed. "If I try to take all five of you in this wagon, we'll be caught for sure. Now, my friend here helps me carry 'packages' like you and your children all the time."

The afternoon rain continued to pour through the pine boughs, and everyone was soaking wet and irritable. Annie studied the two old men, a "Mr. Smith" and a "Mr. Jones," who were arguing with her parents. She knew that the drivers wouldn't tell their real names because they didn't want to be identified if something went wrong. Although their pale white faces were lined with deep wrinkles, and their backs were bent with age, both men seemed strong and very determined. Mama and Papa were losing the argument, and everyone knew it. The two old men were right. It was too dangerous to travel all together in one wagon. It would look very suspicious.

"But we need to be together," Mama cried weakly. "That's why we're running away. We want to be together as a family."

"You'll have all the family time you want when we get you to the North. We'll make sure you find each other up there," he told Mama. Then meeting Papa's eyes, the old man tried to reassure him. "We'll take good care of your family, and so will the people who help you along this secret road that you're about to travel. You've got to trust us."

Papa hesitated while he considered that, and then looked at Isaiah and Annie. Finally he said, "You two will go with 'Mr. Smith' here while your Mama, Jacob, and me will go with his partner. We'll be taking two different routes, but they'll both end in the same place and we'll be together again. Do exactly what he tells you to do, and take care of each other." Papa hugged Annie hard, then released her to throw his arms around his son. "Do whatever you must to take care of yourself and your sister, Isaiah. I'm depending on you." Isaiah nodded, tears filling his eyes. Annie hugged Mama and Jacob, and then gasped as the old man opened up the secret chamber in his wagon.

"It's a false bottom!" she exclaimed. "No one will ever see us there!"

"Annie," the old man said, "take the blankets that you and Isaiah are carrying and lay them on the floorboards. They will help soften the bumps in the road and keep you warm. You'll have to lay flat for the journey, and we have far to go today, but at least you two will have each other for company. Climb in and get yourselves settled."

Annie and Isaiah obediently did as they were told, and Mr. Smith secured the latch on the false bottom. Once the door and latch were covered with the piles of hay the driver had brought, no one would ever suspect that he was carrying illegal cargo.

She could hear the voices of her parents and her little brother as they climbed into the false bottom of the other wagon. She knew that it would be many weeks before her family would all be together again.

"Good-bye, Mama! Good-bye, Papa! Good-bye, Jacob!" Annie whispered as the horses pulled the wagon onto the dirt road, only the first path she would travel on this long and dangerous journey.

5
Nunnahi

The cold rain splattering on his forehead woke John from a fitful sleep. He had tossed and turned on the hard ground all night, dreaming of cruel blue-uniformed soldiers wielding bayonets, and of his parents, long dead. As he tried to sit up, he realized that his stomach was rolling as well, reeling in protest at the undercooked bacon it had been forced to digest last night. The tiny fire Grandfather had built sizzled as each raindrop did its best to extinguish even the smallest flame. John was cold and weary, sick to his stomach, and sick in his spirit. He wanted to go home.

Wrapping his soggy blanket around his shoulders, John pulled himself up off the damp ground. His bones ached, making him feel like an old man, and he moved stiffly. The cold wet weather made his leg feel even worse, and walking had become almost unbearable. Glancing around the compound in the dreary gray dawn, he tried to spot his grandfather.

In the weeks that they had lived in the fort, many more of The People had crowded inside the palisade. There were probably over a hundred now, and Grandfather felt it was his responsibility to look after all of them. He comforted them with the different herbal medicines that he was able to prepare, but still many had died from sickness or the harsh living conditions. Grandfather looked terribly weary himself, and John worried about him.

Spying the older man in one of the makeshift lean-tos that The

People had constructed to afford some protection from the weather, John hobbled painfully in his direction. Grandfather was busily trying to soothe a feverish child with herbal tea. As quickly as he spooned it into her mouth, his little patient spit it right back at him. In spite of his throbbing leg, John had to laugh. Grandfather turned and smiled at the boy.

"I thought you were going to sleep the day away, Grandson!" Gray Hawk teased. Then taking a long, serious look at John's face, he asked, "Is the pain bad today?"

John simply shrugged. "It's tolerable. How can I help you?"

The old man's eyes twinkled. "You can try getting some medicine into this little one. Her name is Singing Brook. I have more of the tea on my face than she has in her mouth!"

John knelt down and took the cup from his grandfather. "Now then, take this tea that my grandfather has prepared for you. It will make you feel so much better."

But the little girl squeezed her lips shut, and refused to do as John told her. Instead, she looked past him to a bright red cardinal perched on a branch directly over John's head.

"Oh, I see. You like the pretty red bird, don't you? Would you like to hear a story about him?" he asked the child. Her eyes brightened and she nodded her head.

"Well," John began soothingly, "one day, a raccoon was passing a wolf deep in the forest. The raccoon kept calling out insults to the wolf, criticizing the wolf's long plain tail while he bragged about his own beautifully striped tail. The wolf soon tired of the raccoon's insults and he turned and chased him. The raccoon was terrified, and began to run away as fast as he could."

The little girl was quickly caught up in the tale, and barely noticed when John slipped a spoonful of tea into her mouth. He continued the story.

"The raccoon spied a tree, and scurried up. He found a nice, long sturdy branch where he could stretch out in the sun and rest, knowing that the wolf could never get him there."

Another spoonful of tea found its way into the little girl's mouth.

"The wolf saw the raccoon in the tree, and circled its trunk three times, but could not figure out how to get the raccoon. Finally tiring of the entire business, the wolf laid down on a nearby creek bank to wait for the raccoon to come down from its perch."

The cup of tea was nearly gone now, and Grandfather grinned from ear to ear as he watched his grandson charm the young patient.

"Wolf stretched out in the sun on the creek bank, and promptly fell asleep. The raccoon, who had been watching the wolf, quietly crept down from the high branch and approached the wolf. Carefully, the raccoon took mud from the creek bank and spread it over the wolf's eyes. Then, he ran away as fast as he could, never to see the wolf again."

The tea was completely gone by now, but the little girl was entranced by John's story, as were her brother, sister, and parents. So he continued. "When the wolf woke up, he was terrified when he could not open his eyes. He began to whine and cry. Along came a little brown bird through the bushes. When he heard the wolf's sad cries, he decided to go see if he could help him. The wolf told the little bird that if he could get his eyes open, he would show him where he'd find some nice red paint to paint himself. The brown bird agreed, and began to peck at the dried mud on the wolf's eyes.

"When the wolf could finally see again, he took the little bird to a rock that had streaks of bright red paint running through it. The bird painted himself with the paint, and he has been a red bird ever since!"

The little group that had assembled to hear John's story laughed and applauded. Their pleasure was short-lived however. Corporal Tidwell, smirking cruelly, came forward with disheartening news.

"Get up! Get ready to move out! We leave today for your new home!" A sickening grin appeared on his face. "Pack up whatever you think you can carry and leave the rest. You won't be coming back here. Old people will ride in the wagons. Young boys and men will walk. You cripple," he said, gesturing at John, "can ride with the old women and babies." Snickering, he turned and sauntered away.

Grandfather tucked his arm around John's shoulders. "So today it begins," he said sadly. "The day we must travel this road of grief, this *nunnahi*, has come at last. Let us gather what we can, and join the others, John. We will walk this road together."

* * *

The cold winter sun did its best to penetrate the tall, gray pines of the Appalachian foothills. Rotten tree branches that had fallen along the trail cracked like dried bones beneath the procession of moccasined feet and slowly turning wagon wheels. A startled drove of gray birds, naturally camouflaged to match their winter home, flitted between the bare hardwoods and green cedars. Weeping Cherokee women sang their mourning songs as they trudged along, chilling John's heart with their bitter notes.

As had been his practice for weeks now, John shuffled along the road beside the wagon carrying his grandfather. Looking behind him, the trail of wagons and walkers curved through the trees and over a gray knoll for as far as he could see. Soldiers on horseback patrolled the march, making certain that none of The People attempted to escape. *As if anyone could,* John thought angrily.

The whining voice of Corporal Tidwell interrupted his thoughts. "They've made room for you in the wagon with the old women, cripple," the soldier taunted John as he pulled his horse up next to him. "They'd be pleased to have one more baby to take care of back there. C'mon, I'll take you."

"Corporal, that will do," ordered another soldier, whose authoritative voice put an immediate end to Tidwell's teasing. John had not seen this man before, but had heard rumors that a new soldier had been sent to take charge of what the white men were now calling "the Cherokee Removal." The commanding demeanor of this man told John that he must be Tidwell's new superior officer. The man was taller and heavier than Tidwell, with salt-and-pepper whiskers trailing down his wrinkled, wind-whipped face. But it wasn't his large stature or his braided gold uniform that impressed John. This man wore his authority, as thick as a bear skin, with dignity and confidence. *This is a man who doesn't need to demand the respect of his soldiers*, John acknowledged silently. *They give it to him willingly.*

"Take two men with you to the town of Murfreesburrough, about two miles up ahead," he ordered Tidwell. "Find someone there who can direct you to the Joiner farm. I've made arrangements to camp there for the night. Make the necessary preparations for the Indians and the horses."

"Yes, sir, Captain Cannon!" Tidwell answered sharply, wheeled his horse around, and rode off briskly. He ignored John as he galloped past, nearly knocking the Indian boy off his feet.

Captain Cannon looked down at John, concern creeping into his gentle eyes. "Are you all right, boy?" he asked kindly. "It's a long walk for any man, but it must be particularly difficult for someone with a troublesome leg."

"I'm fine, Captain," John answered proudly. "I'll walk just as the other young men of my tribe must. I will walk here beside my grandfather, Gray Hawk, in case he needs me."

Captain Cannon smiled at the confident tone in the boy's words. "Of course, young man. Your grandfather must be very pleased to have such a loyal grandson." Turning to the wagon, the captain addressed Gray Hawk.

"It's an honor to meet you, sir. I apologize that it must be under these circumstances." He spread his arms wide, as if to take in all of the shame and sadness of the Cherokee on this terrible trail. "I have heard many reports of your great leadership, and of the respect the people hold for you. It is my sad privilege to accompany you on this journey. If there is anything that you or your noble grandson need, please notify one of the soldiers and they will contact me directly."

Gray Hawk stared squarely into the officer's eyes, but did not speak. Instead, he slowly nodded, and looked away. Captain Cannon touched the brim of his hat lightly, smiled briefly at John, and rode on. The warmth of that small smile, and the respectful way in which the captain had addressed his grandfather, melted just a tiny piece of the bitter ice surrounding John's heart.

6
Hwilahl

The winter sky was gray with dusk when the wagons arrived at the Joiner farm. Weary from the rough roads and cold winds, the Indians fashioned blankets into lean-tos and lit their cooking fires. Soldiers brought around cornmeal and bacon to be cooked for supper, and children carried pails of water from the Joiner's nearby stream.

After finishing their paltry dinner, John and Gray Hawk settled back against the wagon, their blankets pulled closely around their shoulders for warmth. John pulled his flute from his belt, and played softly in the vanishing light. "Good, Grandson," Gray Hawk commented. "You are making music as soothing as your father's. He has shared his talent with you." The warmth of his grandfather's praise glowed in John's heart.

Soon, the winter night settled over the campsite, bringing with it an icy darkness that could never be thawed by the weak flames of the tiny fires dotting the farmland. John shivered, and snuggled closer to his grandfather.

A question tugged at his heart, however, a question that he had wanted to ask again and again, but his grandfather had been so busy, so concerned with the welfare of The People, that John had hesitated to ask it. Now, in his exhaustion and fear, he could wait no longer. It took the form of one word.

"Why?" John asked softly. The tears that he had held inside

for so many months pooled in his eyes. "Why, Grandfather?" he repeated, his voice choking with emotion.

John could not see the old man's face in the growing darkness, but he could feel the familiar arms tighten around his shoulders, and he recognized the coarseness of his grandfather's white hair as he rested his head on his grandson's. Gray Hawk considered John's question for a long time before he spoke. His answer also took the form of one word.

"Greed," he replied sadly. "Greed."

That night John dreamed about his parents and his grandmother. He dreamed that they were sick again with the terrible coughing illness that had caused their deaths and the deaths of many of The People. In the dream, Grandfather was running from forest to field, searching for the medicines that would bring a cure, but he could never find one. John could feel Gray Hawk's pain and frustration even in the dream, and he became anxious with worry. Dreadful storm clouds had gathered over his head in this nightmare, and he could hear the rumbling of thunder, loud and thick in his ears. He tried to run for cover, but in the manner of dreams, he felt himself rooted to the spot where he stood, watching his parents and grandmother die. "Grandfather, Grandfather!" John yelled in his dream, but Gray Hawk simply looked away. Then, without a word, his grandfather went to the pallet where his wife lay, stretched out beside her on the cold, wet ground, and closed his eyes.

Some noise like sharp blasts of thunder, whether real or dream, John couldn't be sure, jarred him awake. His heart was racing with terror as he reached out to feel his grandfather's comforting presence beside him. Snuggling close to the old man, John tried to calm himself. But then, just as his heart began to slow, he heard that noise again, the thunder from his dream, and he realized that it was not thunder, but coughing. A hacking, sickening cough was coming from deep within his grandfather's chest.

So it was there, on a cold dark night somewhere in Tennessee, that John heard the sound that foretold his future and his grandfather's death. Typhus, the terrible disease of fever and coughing, had stolen his mother, his father, and his grandmother. Would it now steal away his grandfather, too?

* * *

The next morning John stayed close to his grandfather, keeping a warm blanket wrapped around the old man's shoulders, and hurrying to get water for him whenever the wagons stopped for a rest. Grandfather noticed John's extra attentiveness, and raised his bushy white eyebrows questioningly as his grandson approached with yet another dipperful of water. Gray Hawk gratefully accepted the water that John offered, and then held on to his hand as the wagon continued to roll slowly forward, in line with the countless others. John limped awkwardly along beside his grandfather, his eyes diverted to the dusty road before him.

"John, why do you busy yourself taking care of me? You get no food or water for yourself, only for your grandfather. Is there something worrying you, like perhaps an old man's wheezing cough?" Gray Hawk struggled to suppress the wracking cough that he had been battling all morning.

John did not answer. He did not look up from the road, for he did not want Gray Hawk to see the fear in his eyes. "My grandson, look at me," his grandfather said gently. "I know what you fear. I understand that you are remembering your parents' death and your grandmother's death. This may be the same illness, or it may just be a sickness that passes quickly on its own. I do not know. My life rests in the hands of the Great Spirit, as does yours. He will guide us and care for us."

In a flash of anger, John looked up into his grandfather's eyes. "Did the Great Spirit care for my mother or father? Did He care for Grandmother? What will happen to me if He chooses to leave me alone with no family?"

"Remember the word 'hwilahl,' my grandson? 'Thou must go.' You must go with The People and care for them. This is your sacred trust as a member of the Blue Clan. Wherever The People live, they will need the ancient medicines and teachings to keep the sacred traditions alive. Hwilahl, John, hwilahl."

* * *

As commanding officer of this Cherokee Removal march, Captain Cannon was expected to keep a log of the significant events of each day. But some days, like today, were very difficult to record because of the despair the words brought to his soul. On this night he wrote the following entry into his journal:

> *January 3, 1839: Weather conditions cold but clear. Company made only two miles today because of sickness and general malaise. Three deaths to report: Buried Nancy Redbird, young daughter of Michael and Ann Redbird; Running Deer, elder; and Bright Skies, mother of two young sons. All three died from fever and fits of coughing, also strange rash. I suspect typhus. Several others are now showing symptoms. Most significantly, Gray Hawk, healer and respected leader of this tribe.*

* * *

The next several days brought harsh winds and bitter cold to the barren landscape. Captain Cannon pushed the weary party to cover as many miles as possible each day, but by the time they crossed the state line from Tennessee into Kentucky, more than fifty of the Cherokee were seriously ill and many more were showing symptoms of disease.

Knowing that he must give the people time to rest, Captain Cannon made arrangements to stop at a farm belonging to Charles and Susannah Thompson, located just outside of Hopkinsville, Kentucky.

At around noon on the day of their arrival in Hopkinsville, snow flurries and icy rain began splattering the sluggish procession, leaving both the Indians and soldiers weary and cold. By sundown, the first of the company's wagons bumped along the ruddy road that led to the low pasture land of the Thompson farm. Later that evening, the flurries had grown into a full-blown blizzard.

The Indians desperately sought protection in the groves of trees that bordered the farm, building makeshift partitions of fallen limbs and blankets around their wagons. The howling winds quickly doused any attempt to ignite even the smallest cooking fire. The only sounds that could be heard above the gale were the coughs and moans of the sick.

Late that night, Captain Cannon wrote this entry in his journal:

January 28, 1839: Buried Alsey Timberlake, infant daughter of James Timberlake. Also, William Whitehead died from fever. Gray Hawk continues to worsen, and the Cherokee are beginning to despair that he may die. They continually look to him for leadership and comfort. Many more sick with symptoms of typhus: cough, fever, rash. Dispensed corn and fodder. Made 7 miles today.

7
Willie's Scheme

The wagon carrying its secret cargo of runaway slaves stopped for the night in a grove of trees just outside of Hopkinsville, Kentucky. It had been an agonizing time for Isaiah and Annie, cramped in their hiding place, frightened and exhausted. Mr. Smith unlatched the secret compartment, and the two youngsters struggled to climb out, their arms and legs stiff and sore from their journey. They had only stopped for brief rest times during the long trip. They had to keep moving, Mr. Smith had explained, because of the slave hunters who could be anywhere, and who would not hesitate to kill the white abolitionist. Then Annie and Isaiah would be taken back to the plantation in chains where they would be beaten severely, or even worse. Annie shuddered at the thought.

The brother and sister huddled close together in the cold night, their backs leaning against a large oak tree. The blankets that had been used to soften the jolts of the rutted roads now warmed their bodies and souls, as they were comforted by memories of their mother sitting in the dim lantern light, carefully sewing each stitch of every seam.

"Isaiah, where do you suppose Mama and Papa are now?" Annie whispered to her brother.

"Probably having a nice warm meal of roast chicken and corn bread in some big house in the North, just waiting for us," Isaiah replied dreamily. "I can almost see them, gathered around a fancy table, eating on real china plates, laughing and celebrating their freedom. Jacob's probably lonesome for you, asking Mama a hundred times every day: 'Where's Annie? Where's Annie?' " His sister smiled at that, and just for a moment, she could imagine the scene that Isaiah had described. So vivid was her imagination, she could almost taste the corn bread.

"Won't it be wonderful to all be together again?" she asked sleepily.

Mr. Smith shattered her happy dreams with his sharp words. "Now, you two wait right here. In the morning you'll see an old white man walking down this road. He'll have a cane in his hand, and a sack thrown over his shoulder. Follow him and he'll lead you to a safe house where your next guide will be waiting. I'll be leaving you here, heading south to pick up more 'packages.' Try to get some sleep, and good luck to you both." After handing them a small sack of food, Mr. Smith hollered a command at the horses and turned his wagon around.

Tiredly, Annie opened the small burlap sack and found it held two hard, dry biscuits and several pieces of the tough jerky Mr. Smith seemed to be so found of. She sighed. They'd eaten little else since they began this trip. After handing a portion of their meager meal to her brother, Annie choked down a bite of the jerky and then bit into the tough biscuit.

"I could do with some of that imaginary corn bread right now," she told her brother.

Isaiah laughed. "Finish up that 'roast chicken' you're eating, and we'll move our blankets further back into the woods where we'll be better hidden. Some unexpected traveler could spot us easily here."

They found a sheltered place in an outcropping of rocks where they could rest unseen, and Annie spread out one blanket on the cold ground. The other blanket they pulled around themselves, and then, nestled together for warmth, they drifted into sleep.

"Well, well, what have we here?" Annie and Isaiah were jarred awake by the loud, piercing voice of a stranger standing over them.

"Willie, come take a look at this!" he yelled. "We got us some runaway slaves, I do believe."

Suddenly eight shotguns were pointed in their direction as the siblings struggled to their feet. Isaiah tried to position himself in front of Annie, his arms outstretched as if to protect her.

Pushing through the circle of men, Willie Hall spoke. "Why, I believe you're right. Now, what are you two doing out here?"

Shivering with fear but determined to appear brave, Isaiah answered him, "We're not bothering anybody. We're traveling through, just like you and your men, and we decided to stop here for the night. We don't have any money for a room," Isaiah said pointedly, "so we had to stay out here in the woods."

"No money, is that right? Well, me and my boys might be able to help you out with that. Isn't that right, boys?" Willie smiled at his gang then, and they responded with smirks and quiet laughter, nodding their heads and mumbling their agreement. "Get a fire going, Davey," Willie briskly ordered one of the men. "Bring some food over here. I'm sure you two are hungry, aren't you?"

Isaiah would not be fooled by Willie Hall's attempt at friendliness. "What do you want with me and my sister?" he demanded, still maintaining his protective posture around Annie.

"Now just settle down," Willie replied. "I'm not going to hurt you or your sister here. I'm no slave catcher. I have a business deal for you that might help put a few pennies in my pocket and yours. Come over here by the fire, sit down and listen. If you don't like my plan, I'll take my men and leave."

Hesitantly, Isaiah and Annie picked up their blankets and moved closer to the fire. Annie had to admit that its warmth was a welcome relief on this bitter cold night. She and Isaiah had been too frightened to start one, fearful that a slave catcher might see it. It seems they'd been discovered anyway, she thought bitterly.

"Tell your men to put their guns away," Isaiah told Willie, "then we can talk." Willie motioned to his men, and the shotguns disappeared. It was then that Annie noticed the strange bandage on Willie's thumb, dark red blood visible through the dirty gauze. She decided she didn't really want to know what had happened to him and so remained silent.

"This is the plan," Willie began. "I've done this at least a dozen times so far, and it's met with success each time. Now, you look like a strong, healthy man. What's your name, boy?"

"Isaiah, and this is Annie," Isaiah replied.

"All right, Isaiah, this is what I propose. Plantations around here are always looking for good, healthy slaves. I happen to know that there's a plantation not far from here that will pay a fair price for a strong back." He paused, and poked the fire with a stick causing it to flame up quickly. "To save Master Stuart Cooper a trip to the slave auction, I'll take you to the plantation, and sell you to him."

Annie gasped in horror, and Isaiah jumped to his feet. "Sell me!" he shouted, "I'm running away from slavery! What kind of business deal is this?"

"Calm down, Isaiah," Willie said softly. "You didn't let me finish. In a week or so, I'll send my men to come steal you back. We'll split the money I get for selling you, and you and your sister continue on your way north. The money will be real useful to you when you get to the end of your journey."

"How do I know that I can trust you?" Isaiah asked suspiciously.

"You don't," Willie replied. "But if I'm telling you the truth, and I swear on my mother's grave that I am, you and your sister stand to make a lot of money. A young, strong Negro like yourself, Isaiah, would easily bring over one hundred dollars from any plantation owner. That's fifty dollars clear profit for you and your sister to spend when you get to wherever it is that you're headed." Willie let Isaiah consider the offer for a few minutes.

Finally, Isaiah asked, "What about Annie? I don't want her involved. It sounds too dangerous." Annie bristled at that, but Isaiah silenced her with a stern look.

"Annie wouldn't bring much money anyway. Owners won't pay much for girls. They want young bucks like you to do the hard work. Get her hidden away someplace safe for a few days, and when this is all over you can go get her and continue on your way, a good bit richer for your trouble!"

Willie made it all sound so simple that Isaiah felt foolish to refuse. "All right," Isaiah conceded reluctantly. "I'll get Annie to the next safe house, and then double back here." Shocked, Annie stared at her brother in amazement. Her brother was actually agreeing to this terrifying scheme!

"Meet me back here day after tomorrow at dawn," said Willie. "I'll be waiting at the rocks."

Once Willie and his gang had left them, Annie battered her brother with questions. "What am I supposed to do while you're gone? How do we know that we can trust this man? What if he doesn't come get you? What would Mama and Papa want you to do?" Annie could not hide her terror from her brother.

Finally, Isaiah had enough of her questioning. The words he spoke were gentle, but his voice was firm. "Annie, I'm doing what I think is best for both of us. We'll need that money when we get to the North, and remember, Papa told me to take care of you. That's what I'm doing. You can stay at the safe house until I come for you. You'll only have to wait a week or so. Now, try to get some sleep. It's almost dawn."

Annie couldn't sleep. She tossed and turned on the cold hard ground, until the first wisps of morning light drifted through the trees. "It's time to meet our guide," Isaiah told her, stretching stiff muscles as he got to his feet. Annie could see that he had not slept much either. His eyes looked tired, and he was moving slowly, like an old man. "Gather up the blankets, Annie, and meet me at the road."

Folding up the quilts, Annie voiced a silent prayer that God would take care of her brother today, and that He would protect the rest of her family, too, wherever they were.

* * *

"I saw them, sir," Michael told Master Ellidge as they stood on the back veranda of the main house. "The two older children went in one wagon, while the mama, papa, and baby were put in the other. They're running away to the North sure enough, just like I told you."

"Good work, Michael," Master Ellidge praised his overseer. "I'll take care of it from here. I know some men in town who will be only too happy to bring those runaways back here where they belong. You'll be properly rewarded." With a wave of the master's hand, Michael was dismissed.

The overseer returned to his cabin, a wicked smile pasted on his face. He'd known about their plan the whole time. He'd listened outside their cabin that evening as they made their plans, and then he had followed them through the woods to the waiting wagons. *They thought they'd get away*, he mused with a smirk, *leaving me to do the extra work, getting me in trouble with the master. I took care of them, didn't I?*

* * *

The Alabama sky was a maelstrom of swirling black clouds streaked with sharp spears of lightning. In the pounding rain, Master Ellidge's slave catcher cruelly dragged his prey back to the plantation. Papa, his hands tied together, was pulled along behind a horse whose rider took great delight in seeing his prisoner stumble and fall. The slave catcher let the horse drag the man on his belly down the muddy, rock-strewn road, while his bawling woman and her screaming brat struggled to get him to his feet. One time she fell, too, and the slave catcher laughed as both woman and baby stumbled into a pool of mud. Finally the horse stopped behind the master's house, and the slave catcher dismounted.

"I've brought back your property, Mister Ellidge," the man called out. The master came out the door then, and grabbed the rope binding the slave's hands. "Where are the others?" he demanded. "I've paid you well for your services. I expect to see the other two before the end of the week. Do you understand?"

"Yes, sir," the man replied mounting his weary horse. Little Jacob, tired and hungry, cried again as the slave catcher trotted away.

"Woman, quiet that child!" the Master barked at her. Yanking the rope that still bound Papa's hands, he led the exhausted slave down to the whipping post. There, he stripped off what was left of the man's shirt, and secured his arms. Michael appeared, handing his master the whip.

Mama covered Jacob's eyes so that he could not see what was happening to his father, but she could not shut out the screams of pain that were heard by every slave on the plantation. Master Ellidge was sending a message to his property: *If you run, you will be caught. And you will be punished.*

8

A Secret in Black and White

The morning sun had snaked its way almost to the top branches of the oak trees when Annie and Isaiah spied an old man coming down the road. To their surprise, they could see that the man was limping. He was hunched over a large stick, leaning on it for support as he slowly tottered down the road. As he neared the runaways, Annie and Isaiah saw long white hair spilling out from under his battered cap. His jacket was torn and ragged, held together in the front by several mismatched buttons. He seemed so weak and fragile that Annie thought he must surely be at least one hundred years old. "I hope the safe house isn't too far or he'll never get us there!" she whispered to her brother. Isaiah looked concerned.

Limping awkwardly toward the two children, he growled at them. "Get back in the trees. Do you want some slave catchers to see you?" Hastily, Annie and Isaiah ducked behind some bushes. To their amazement, the old man tossed down his stick and quickly followed them into the thicket. Crouching low next to them, the man took off his cap, and Annie gasped in surprise when his white hair came off, too!

The man grinned. "Pretty good disguise, wouldn't you say? I always fancied myself an actor!" Winking at Annie he said, "Had you fooled, didn't I, little one? I wear this," he gestured to the cap with the white hair attached to the inside seam, "just in case I'm spotted by some unfriendly travelers. Even slave catchers won't

50

bother with an 'old man' like me!" Studying the man closely, Annie realized that without the cap and the hunched-over appearance, the man appeared to be quite young, maybe just thirty years of age or so.

He continued, "You may call me Charles. My wife Susannah and I live in the house that will be your next stop. It's not far. I'm going to be walking on the road, but you need to stay in the woods and follow me from there. It won't be an easy walk for you, but my 'limp' gives me an excuse for traveling slowly. Make sure you watch me, and hide quickly if I should meet anyone on the road."

Nodding, the pair moved deeper into the woods, making sure that they could still see their guide. Charles picked up his cap and his walking stick. Playing the old man once again, he began the taxing journey to the farmhouse where he and his wife, Susannah, hid slaves who were traveling north to freedom. Charles had no idea, however, the changes that these two special runaways would bring to his life.

Several hours later, Annie and Isaiah spied a large farmhouse at the top of a grassy hill. The house was two stories tall, painted a stark white with simple black shutters on the glass-paned windows. In a vibrant wave of welcome, several brightly colored quilts and blankets moved gently in the breeze as they hung on the rope line in the side yard. Charles joined Annie and Isaiah in the woods and led them up a narrow path toward the back of the house. Removing his cap and jacket, he tucked them in a crevice between two large rocks. He leaned his walking stick against a tree and instructed the pair to wait while he opened the cellar door.

When Charles was certain that no one was watching, he motioned for Isaiah and Annie to follow him down the cellar steps. Once they were safely inside, he pulled the heavy twin doors closed behind him. Annie welcomed the sheltering arms of darkness, feeling at ease for the first time in this long journey.

Charles led the runaways through a tiny door at the end of what seemed to be the cellar's rock wall. Entering the room first, he lit a small kerosene lantern. "Why it's a false wall!" Isaiah cried admiringly. "This little room is hidden so well by the rocks, no one would even know that it's here!" Annie was pleased to see two cots set against the wall. *I'll be sleeping on a real bed tonight!* She nearly clapped her hands with joy. The room was cool, but dry, and she smiled contentedly, happy to finally have four walls around her and a roof over her head. Almost hidden in the semi-darkness in the corner of the room was a narrow spiral staircase. Suddenly a light appeared at the top of the stairs, and a feminine voice called down softly, "Charles, are you there?"

"Susannah, come down and meet our guests. Bring some food and water, too, for I suspect that they are almost as hungry as your starving husband!"

Moving gracefully down the wooden steps in her long full skirt, Susannah Thompson carried a large tray bearing three steaming bowls of soup and a warm loaf of bread. She was a tall, slender woman with dark brown hair pulled into a sleek bun at the nape of her neck. Annie happily breathed in the appetizing aroma of the food Mrs. Thompson carried, and her stomach growled its approval.

Charles Thompson said a brief prayer of thanks for their safe journey and this wonderful meal before the three travelers began devouring the delicious food. Susannah laughed as the trio gobbled everything on the tray. "Would you like some more?" she asked, smiling.

Isaiah replied shyly, "If it's not too much trouble, ma'am. This is the best meal we've had since the last time we ate our Mama's cooking."

"Why, young man, that's a lovely compliment. I'll be right back." With that, she picked up the men's empty bowls, and carried the tray back up the steps to her kitchen. Annie continued eating, savoring every bit of the first hot meal she'd had in weeks.

Charles went over to the small stove that stood in the middle of the room. Using the flame of the lantern, he lit a piece of kindling and placed it in the stove. Annie could see that the stove's pipe went straight up into the ceiling, and she stopped gulping her soup just long enough to look questioningly at Charles.

"It's all right, Annie. I've fixed the pipe so that the smoke from this fire goes through the ceiling right into the main fireplace in the kitchen. As long as we have a fire going up there, no one could ever tell that there is a fire down here. This way, we can keep all of our special cellar guests warm and comfortable."

Annie smiled. "Do you get a lot of visitors like my brother and me?" she asked.

"Susannah and I have shepherded several runaways like you two on their way to freedom. Our work here is very important, but it's also very secret." Charles moved back to the cot, where he sat down next to Annie. "You two will rest here for several days until arrangements can be made for the next leg of your journey. You must stay hidden in this cellar, however, for our pastures are about to become very crowded." Charles shook his head sadly before continuing, "Cherokee Indians are being forcibly removed from their homeland to the south and east. Our government is sending them to a reservation in Oklahoma, and they will be passing through our town of Hopkinsville tomorrow. Over a thousand will arrive here on our farm, and Susannah and I will be busy seeing to their needs."

Even though her mouth was stuffed with Mrs. Thompson's delicious freshly baked bread, Annie could not contain her curiosity. "A thousand Indians? Right here?" she asked, swallowing hard. "I saw an Indian family one time when the overseer took Mama and me to the market at Florence. I'd never seen anyone like them before. Their little girl had the longest black hair I ever saw. Mama had to poke me to keep me from staring." She stopped chattering long enough to drink some cool water that Mrs. Thompson had brought back down the steps with her. The woman placed two more bowls of steaming soup on the tiny table.

Susannah smiled at her. "Charles and I were teachers at a school that taught reading and writing to the Cherokee. We're hoping that we will know some of the people that arrive here tomorrow. How wonderful it would be to see our Indian friends again, but how sad that it is has to be under these circumstances." Susannah's face grew dark with concern. "You see, Annie, they've been forced to leave behind everything they loved. Many have become sick. Some have even died. It's been a long, terrible journey for them, and I hope that we can bring them some comfort while they're here with us. In fact, we came to this farm just a few months ago because we knew that the Cherokees would be passing through this way, and we wanted to help them any way that we could."

Charles continued his wife's story while Susannah gathered blankets for her guests. "Our friend, Homer McManus, owned this farm until recently. He had become very ill, and asked if Susannah and I would like to take over the land and his position of conductor on the Underground Railroad. We couldn't refuse."

Annie had many questions that she wanted to ask about the Indians, but Charles placed his hand on her shoulder to quiet her.

"We'll talk more tomorrow, Annie. It's time that you and Isaiah get some rest," he said, as he rose to his feet.

"You must tell us now if you know of any thing else that you might need before morning. You must be completely silent while you are here with us. We will not be coming back down to the cellar tonight," he paused for a moment, choosing his words carefully. "Children, there are dangerous men out there, men who are bent on catching slaves and taking them back to their masters. They must not know that you two are here. If they find you, it would mean imprisonment for my wife and me, and terrible punishment for you. Do you both understand?"

Isaiah and Annie, their faces solemn, nodded their heads, and Charles gave them a smile. "Get a good night's rest, you two," he said as he and Susannah climbed the stairs to the kitchen, closing the door behind them.

A few minutes later, while the siblings rested on their cots, Annie could sense that her brother was deep in thought about Willie

Hall's offer. In the dim lantern light, she studied his face before she spoke. "Isaiah," she whispered, "are you still planning on going to meet those men? We're safe here, and the Thompsons are going to take good care of us. We don't need Willie Hall's money. Please, Isaiah, stay here with me."

But Annie could tell by the look in his eyes that Isaiah had already made up his mind. She'd seen that same look in her father's eyes when he had made up his mind about something and wouldn't be budged, no matter what Mama said to him. "Be patient, Annie," Mama would say. "Your Papa is a stubborn man, but he's smart. He'll do what's right."

When people talked about Papa and Isaiah, they always said things like, 'The apple doesn't fall far from the tree.' Annie hoped that they were right. She prayed that Isaiah was just as smart as their papa.

"Annie, I have to go," Isaiah said gently. "The money I get will mean a new start for our whole family. You stay here with the Thompsons and wait for me. I'll be back in a few days." Then he hugged her so hard she thought she might break in two. "I love you, Annie," he whispered.

"I love you, too, Isaiah," she replied. Annie curled up on her cot, and tried to stay awake, but the bed was too soft and warm and she couldn't resist closing her eyes. Soon, she was lost in a deep sleep.

Isaiah waited until far into the night before he carefully opened the cellar door leading to the side yard. Stepping into the brutally cold winter air was a shock after the warmth of the cellar. He was thankful for the blanket he'd brought with him, and he pulled it more tightly around his shoulders. Tonight the full moon was dipping in and out of cottony clouds, but still it provided enough light for Isaiah to find the trail through the woods. Isaiah could see a dim circle around the moon, a sure sign that snow was on the way. He recognized the outcropping of rocks where Charles had hidden his disguise, and he continued past that to the main road. Isaiah's lean form moved stealthily, staying in the shadows but he always kept one eye on the road so that he didn't become hopelessly lost in the woods. Finally, just as the sun began to make its ascent over the horizon, he heard a voice call to him from the woods. "Isaiah, over here!" He knew immediately that Willie Hall and his men were waiting for him, just beyond a stand of trees to his left.

"I hope I'm not making the biggest mistake of my life," Isaiah muttered as he climbed up the hill to meet them.

9
Fool's Gold

"Annie, where's Isaiah? Annie, wake up! Where is your brother?" Susannah shook the girl awake, her words running together in Annie's sleepy brain.

"What, Miss Susannah? What are you talking about? He's in his bed, right over there!" replied Annie, but when she looked, she could see that Isaiah's bed was neatly made, blankets folded and placed on top of the pillow. No one had slept there last night.

"Oh, no!" was all that Annie could say before tears rolled down her cheeks. *How could Isaiah have left me here? Will I ever see him again?*

"Annie," Susannah sat down next to her on the cot, putting her arm around the young girl's shoulder. "Where has Isaiah gone? You must know something. Tell me so that I can help you."

Encouraged by Susannah's comforting words, Annie tears stopped, and she took a deep breath before telling the entire story.

"Isaiah thought that the money would be a great help to us when we get to the North. He thought that Mama and Papa would be proud of him for tricking the slave owner out of fifty dollars. But I think that it's a terrible plan, Miss Susannah.

"The man, Willie Hall, talked about taking him to a plantation owned by Stuart Cooper. Do you know him, Miss Susannah? Can you and Mr. Charles help us? Please?"

Annie's tear-streaked face melted Susannah's heart. Trying to hide her own fear, Miss Susannah smiled weakly and patted the girl's knee. "I'll speak to Charles, Annie, and we'll see what we can do." She patted the young girl's knee. "I brought you some breakfast. There's fresh water in the basin, and the chamber pot is in the corner by the door where you came in. I'll be back as soon as I can." Susannah hurried up the stairs to the kitchen, eager to talk to Charles about Isaiah.

Annie washed herself with the soap and water Susannah had left her. She tried to eat the fragrant porridge and warm biscuits on the tray by her cot, but she found that she couldn't swallow more than a bite or two. Her fear, an enormous rock in the pit of her stomach, made eating impossible. She felt helpless, shut away in the semidarkness of the cellar, all alone.

Wrapping herself in a warm shawl, Susannah ran to the barn where she found Charles, tending to his chores. "You know, Susannah," he said without looking up from his work in the stalls, "I was hoping to get rid of some of those stumps in the back field before the Cherokee arrived. We're going to need the extra acreage for corn this spring," he shook his head, musing. "When am I ever going to find the time now? No one knows how long the Cherokee will need to stay here. This cold weather is making for dangerous travel. And if we should have a blizzard . . ."

Susannah, growing impatient, blurted out, "Isaiah is gone, Charles. Annie thinks he's involved in a scheme to make some money by allowing himself to be sold back into slavery." She shared the details of Annie's story with her husband. " She's worried sick about him and so am I. What can we do?"

Charles leaned heavily on his pitchfork and sighed deeply. "Foolish boy," he muttered. "Trying to get rich quick, and now he's put us all in danger. There's nothing that we can do about it right now, not with a thousand Cherokee due here at sundown." He spoke quietly to Susannah before getting back to his work. "Tell Annie that she'll have to be patient. I'll try to find out what I can in the next few days."

* * *

Willie bound Isaiah's hands with one end of a thick, coarse rope. The other end he tied to the horn of his saddle. "We'll go nice and slow, Isaiah," he told the boy. "We're in no hurry. Stuart Cooper's money ain't going anywhere." He mounted his horse, and Isaiah felt the tug on the rope as Willie nudged the mare forward. Only Isaiah and Willie were making this trip.

The rest of his gang was going to wait in a clearing just off the main road until Willie returned. "Deals like this one are better handled man to man," he'd explained to Isaiah.

As the journey went on, the ropes bit into Isaiah's wrists, and he asked why they were necessary. "We've got to make this look real," Willie had explained. *Does it take blood all over my hands and wrists to make this look real?* Isaiah wondered.

By mid-afternoon, the pale winter sun had hidden itself behind a mass of gray clouds, and the wind was blowing in earnest. Isaiah did not remember ever being so cold. One of Willie's gang, a man named Davey, had taken the boy's blanket because, he reasoned, no runaway would have such a nice, warm quilt to wrap around his sorry bones. As Isaiah was leaving their camp, struggling to stay on his feet behind Willie's horse, he looked back just in time to see Davey wrap the blanket around his shoulders. He smirked at Isaiah, then settled himself by the fire.

Finally, as the first flakes of snow were spitting from the dreary sky, the pair arrived at the Cooper plantation. Isaiah noticed right away that the main house and the outbuildings were in terrible disrepair. Farm equipment littered the barren fields. *Master Stuart Cooper certainly doesn't care much for his farm,* Isaiah concluded. *He probably cares even less for his slaves.*

Willie dragged his captive around to the back of the main house and dismounted. Knocking loudly on the back door, he waited until a house maid appeared. "Get your master, girl. I got some merchandise here he might be interested in purchasing." The maid answered, "Yes, sir," and closed the door.

A few minutes later, Stuart Cooper emerged, bundled in a huge overcoat and wearing a large brown hat that he wore pulled down over shaggy gray hair. He carried an ancient shotgun in his hand. "What have you got there, Willie? Another 'bargain' for me to buy? I swear I don't know how you keep talking these runaways into this ridiculous scheme of yours." Cooper laughed as he walked down the back steps to inspect Isaiah. "Looks like you got a strong one this time, though. The last one I bought from you didn't make it a year. Died of fever before I got my money's worth. This one should do better," he said as he eyed Isaiah up and down. Now the snow was tumbling from the sky in a whirl of icy wind, and Isaiah shivered uncontrollably as Mr. Cooper examined him carefully. "I'll give you seventy-five dollars for him," he announced finally. "That's twenty-five dollars less because of the money I lost on the last slave." Cooper took some coins from his deep pocket, and counted them out.

Willie started to protest, but then decided to accept the offer. Nodding his head, he said, "Fine, it's a deal, and now we're square. Next time I'll expect the full price." Turning to Isaiah, Willie snickered disdainfully at the young man. "You see this money I got here, boy?" he taunted, waving the coins in Isaiah's face. "Well, I call this fool's gold. You're the fool, all right, and I get the gold."

With a mean laugh, he untied Isaiah's hands and gathered up the rope. "Did you actually believe I'd come back and get you? Seventy-five dollars is less than I wanted, but it'll keep me and my gang in whiskey for a while."

Climbing back on his horse, he tipped his hat to Stuart Cooper. His last words to Isaiah chilled the boy more than any blizzard could ever do. "Don't worry about your sister, boy," he sneered. "Maybe I'll have her here with you before you know it!" Then without a backwards glance, he rode off into the swirling snow, leaving Isaiah on Cooper's plantation, a slave once more.

* * *

The silence and darkness of the cellar proved to be more than Annie could bear. Susannah had brought her soup for lunch but did not have time to stay and talk because of the final preparations she was making for the Cherokee's arrival. "It's becoming a real blizzard out there, Annie. They're going to need shelter from the storm, and extra hot food."

"Please, Miss Susannah, let me help," Annie begged. "I worked in the kitchen on the plantation, and I know how to scrub pots and clean floors. Couldn't you use an extra pair of hands?" She knew for sure that she couldn't stand another minute in the cellar alone, worrying about Isaiah.

Reluctantly, Susannah gave in to Annie's pleading. "I don't expect we'll have any visitors today in this terrible storm," she replied slowly, "and, you're right, I could use the help. We'll leave the door at the top of the stairs open, just in case. Listen carefully, and if you hear any strange noises, you must get back down here quickly."

Annie nodded, and climbed the steep, narrow stairs behind Miss Susannah. Once in the kitchen, Annie could see that the cellar door slid back into a recess in the wall when it was opened. When the little door was closed, it matched the paneled room seamlessly and would be difficult for anyone to detect. The two set to work in the kitchen, chopping vegetables and stirring huge pots of broth.

"This will never be enough for everyone," lamented Susannah, "but at least I can feed it to those that are sickly. It might help to strengthen them."

Annie had never worked harder, even on the plantation, and the older woman smiled at the young girl. "Thank you, Annie, for helping. I really couldn't have done all of this without you."

Although Annie had been too busy to pay much attention to the storm outside, the howling winds whipping the walls and roof of the farmhouse now made her hurry to the kitchen window. "Miss Susannah, I've never seen so much snow. The poor Cherokee!" she said, and then thought, *Poor Isaiah! Where is he now? What is happening to my brother?*

Peering through the window to the side yard, Annie could

barely make out splotches of color blowing in the blustering wind. "Miss Susannah, your beautiful quilts are going to be ruined! Besides, my mama always told me that it was bad luck to leave laundry on the clothes line in a storm. Wouldn't you like for me to go gather them up for you?"

"No, Annie," Susannah replied sharply. "Those quilts must remain on the line no matter what. You see, the triangle pattern is a kind of signal to runaways like you, to let them know that this is a safe haven. Even the black and white paint on the house has a secret meaning. Slaves who see a house painted like ours know that they are welcome here."

Suddenly, the danger that the Thompsons were facing became very clear to Annie, and she regarded Miss Susannah with awe. "You and Mr. Charles are putting yourselves at great risk to help me, aren't you?" She looked down at the floor, ashamed. "My brother's actions have put you in even more danger, and I am so sorry. I hope that some day I will be able to repay you for all that you have done for us."

"Just make a wonderful life for yourself, Annie," Susannah lifted the girl's face gently and looked deeply into her eyes. "That's all the payment that Charles and I could ever ask for." Pulling her close, Susannah hugged her warmly, then said, "All right, Annie, now it's time we get back to work!"

Smiling, the two returned to their cooking, side by side in the snug kitchen while the storm raged outside.

10
Aboard *The Sinon*

The sharp blast of the whistle left no doubt that the steamship, *The Sinon*, was making ready to leave the dock. The ancient-looking paddle wheeler, black and white paint peeling from its hull, was loaded down this cold January day with merchant goods from the areas all around southern Illinois.

Hastily grabbing his tattered carpet bag from the wooden bench where he'd been napping in the sun, the young lawyer, Abraham Lincoln, ran to the gangplank. His long, lean frame quickly mounted the ramp to the deck of the ship. His only welcome was a curt nod from a dockhand.

"Almost sailed without you," barked a gruff voice from behind him. "If you'll excuse me, I need to get to the wheelhouse." The old man pushed past Abraham toward the bow of the ship, and disappeared through a narrow door. The loud closing of the door punctuated the end of their conversation.

"Quite a welcome," Abraham chuckled to himself. Lincoln heard the engines firing in earnest now, and he saw clouds of black smoke belch from the ship's towering smokestacks as the boat pulled sluggishly away from the dock. The huge paddle wheel slowly turned in the choppy waters of the Mississippi River.

Struggling to find his sea legs beneath him, Abraham made his way up the main staircase to his room. The hallway he stumbled down was in complete disrepair. The walls were in desperate need of paint, and the floors were scuffed and marked from the hundreds of shoes and boots that had traveled their surfaces. Shifting his bulky satchel to his other hand, Abraham laughed at his own foolishness for hauling such a load on this voyage. He had very few belongings, but he never left his home without his beloved law books. *Eating, sleeping, and reading these books are my three loves*, he grinned, *but not necessarily in that order!*

He laughed, too, at the clever way his landlady, Miriam Hall, had coerced him into taking this trip to help her son Willie. Since being assigned to ride the Illinois eighth judicial circuit as a traveling lawyer, Abraham had not spent much time at the boarding house that the Widow Hall managed. Mostly he stayed only overnight at the large, two-story home, but he had taken several days in late September to help her paint the house. Abraham really hadn't thought the painting was necessary, but Mrs. Hall insisted that the formerly cream-colored building be changed to a bright white, and the handsome blue trim be covered up with an austere black.

Just as Abraham had been convinced to do the widow's bidding with the painting, he had also been persuaded to help her son. He still wasn't quite sure how he'd been talked into traveling all the way down to Cape Girardeau to give legal advice to a suspected horse thief, who probably was guilty of all the charges against him. Willie Hall's reputation in the community, even as a young boy, had not been complimentary. Although his mother had dutifully dragged him to Sunday services at the local Methodist church each week, he had been branded a ne'er-do-well early on. He'd been known to steal anything from the change in his mother's purse to the apples at the local grocery.

One story that was told about Willie had to do with a Baptist preacher and a bucket of soot. Once every three or four months, the Baptists would all gather on Sunday night for a foot-washing service. Willie, only eight years old at the time, along with a few of his young buddies watched as the Baptists removed their shoes, leaving them on the front steps of the church until after the service.

Willie had brought a bucket of soot from his fireplace at home, and very gently filled each of the worshippers' shoes with the black powder. After the service, the Baptists came out to reclaim their footwear. By the time they got home, the churchgoers had feet blacker than a potbellied stove, and Willie's career in crime had begun.

Mrs. Hall refused to accept that her sweet Willie could grow up to be a criminal. And like a mother lioness protecting her young, Miriam would not give up even though her son was now a grown man. "Willie is a good boy, underneath it all. The Bible says, 'Train up a child in the way he should go and when he is old he will not turn from it.' Well, even though his father passed away when he was just a baby, I raised him right. He just got in with that bunch of outlaws down in Kentucky, and they led him astray," Miriam insisted. "My Willie would never do anything wrong. Please help him, Abraham. You're the only man I know with any kind of legal training at all. Bring him home to me, Abraham."

Day after day after day, Miriam pleaded with Abraham, until she wore down his resistance. Finally, on this past Sunday, the landlady had played her trump card. She cooked an enormous meal consisting of all Abraham's favorite foods: fried chicken, warm buttermilk biscuits, and freshly baked chocolate cake.

"Whoever said that a way to a man's heart is through his stomach really knew what he was talking about," Abraham had joked, as he finally consented to make the long trip from Springfield to Quincy by carriage, and then on to Cape Girardeau by the steamship, *The Sinon*. Miriam had happily made the travel arrangements. It was still a mystery to him why she had booked passage for him aboard such a dilapidated ship when there were so many newer, better-maintained vessels available.

But still, that is how Abraham Lincoln, brand-new lawyer and representative from the great state of Illinois, found himself aboard the aging steamship, *The Sinon*, on this very cold winter day in 1839.

After depositing his valise in the tiny state room, Abraham made his way to the dining room for an early supper before retiring to his books for the evening. Like the rest of the ship, the dining room was shabby. It was a small room, with seating for only a few passengers at rickety wooden tables. Stuffing peeked from worn upholstery on the chairs, and dust motes swirled around the tattered draperies. Pale, evening sunlight struggled to provide light through smeared, cracked windows. Smoky oil lamps had been set on the tables, but their dim light only added to the depressing atmosphere. Lincoln helped himself to the sparse offerings of bread, beans, and beef stew, and strode to a nearby table where he sat alone.

Before long, another gentleman entered the room, and Abraham recognized him as the man who had pushed past him earlier. He was a fairly large man, rotund and gray-headed, wearing a worn blue captain's uniform and matching frayed cap. Spying Abraham, he made his way over and settled himself at the same table.

"Hope you don't mind," the man said brusquely. "I just needed to get my dinner before I begin the night watch. I'm the captain of this vessel, Thomas Richardson." He shot out a calloused hand toward Abraham, who shook it vigorously.

"I'm Abraham Lincoln from Springfield. Pleased to make your acquaintance," Lincoln haltingly replied as he struggled to swallow the lumps of dry bread that had somehow managed to lodge themselves in his throat.

"Here, take a gulp or two of this," the captain replied as he passed him a cup of hot tea. "This will cure whatever ails you. Been drinking it since I was just a tiny lad in Carolina. My mother told me that it would cure anything that ailed the body, and I believe she was right. Never been sick a day in my life. And it certainly helps this awful stew go down easier."

Abraham gratefully accepted the tea, and drank it straight down. It was a wonderful concoction of cinnamon and honey, and soothed his throat instantly.

"Thank you," he said, and then remarked with a grin, "You don't seem like the tea drinking kind, if you don't mind my saying so."

Captain Richardson's weathered face broke into a smile. "Never touch the hard liquor. I've seen too many ships brought down by a captain or crew who loved their whiskey. I know this ship isn't the beauty she once was, but she's all I got. I can't afford to lose her to the siren song of alcohol!" Captain Richardson paused to take a huge bite of potato from the steaming stew before him. "Are you a student of the Greek myths, Abraham?"

"Not really, sir," Lincoln replied, continuing his meal. The works of William Shakespeare and the poetry of Robert Burns were more to his liking.

"Ah, but you should be! There's much to learn from those dead, dusty old Greeks! According to one ancient story, the sirens were lovely women that made beautiful but dangerous music to attract sailors. The songs could actually cause the crew to crash their ships upon the rocky shores of the sirens' secret lairs. Once entranced by the magic of the women's songs, the sailors were easily captured and then promptly devoured by the women." Captain Richardson paused, poked his fork around in the stew, and finally skewered a tender bit of meat.

Abraham's jaw hit the table as his spoon clattered to the floor. He stared at the captain in disbelief. "Did you just say that those women *ate* the sailors?"

"Aye," Captain Richardson responded calmly. He chewed his stew thoughtfully before responding. "I suppose the lesson there would be that some things that might seem very attractive should be avoided, or bad consequences will result. Wouldn't you agree, Mr. Lincoln?"

Abraham let out a long, deep breath before he replied. "I would have to agree with you there, Captain," he said, nodding his head. A grin spread across his long, narrow face.

11

The Oracle

Several days later, after many stops at small towns and ports along the way, *The Sinon* finally docked in the bustling city of St. Louis on the Missouri side of the Mississippi River. From his perch on the upper deck, Abraham could see the dock area, its narrow riverside streets choked with booths and stalls where vendors sold their goods to the disembarking steamship passengers. *Time for a walk, just to stretch these long legs of mine,* he thought. *Maybe I'll find a little bauble to give to the Widow Hall to mark my visit to St. Louis.*

With only those thoughts in mind, Lincoln made his way down the staircase to the gangplank and from there into the busy maze of merchants eager to market their wares. Abraham meandered from booth to booth, gazing at the merchandise, ignoring the hawkers and peddlers who yelled their prices and promises at passersby.

Abraham found himself strangely drawn to an odd-looking stall nearly hidden in a side alley. The front of the booth was draped with sheer rainbow-colored cloths, and a strangely sweet fragrance poured from smoking brass pots that were placed intermittently on the ground. Peering through the cloths, Abraham saw a woman sitting at a table, turning over large, colorful cards one by one. As Abraham watched, the woman spoke without moving her eyes from her cards. "Come in, young man," she said, her voice melodious with the accent of the Caribbean.

She was very slender, Abraham noted, even though her frame

was nearly swallowed by the patterned fabrics of gold, purple, and red that she wore. She had adorned herself with an odd assortment of necklaces, bracelets, and rings. Her age was a mystery; her rich ebony skin was very smooth and youthful, but her dark eyes were full of the wisdom of the ages. She could have been twenty, or maybe three times that age. Her hair was wrapped in a colorful headdress made of blue and green silk, and she wore large hoops of bright, shiny copper in her ears. She seemed to Abraham to be very rich, and yet very poor at the same time. *What an odd contradiction she is,* he mused.

"Would you like for me to do a reading for you, sir?" she asked politely in her low, lilting voice. Walking into the booth, Abraham sat down in a rickety chair facing her. "Give me your hand. I believe I have much to tell you." She looked deeply into his eyes, and for just an instant, Abraham saw a flash of concern cross her face. His curiosity aroused, Abraham placed his hand in hers.

The fortune-teller studied the lines on his palm. She traced each mark on his hand with her long, lean finger, as if the lines were a road map, and she was following the pathway of his life.

"Ah, Abraham, you are a man destined for great works and great sorrows. You will find love, I see, but it will come at a dear price," she paused for a moment, considering the crease in the very center of his hand. "Violence will scar the later years of your life," she murmured, and as Abraham watched in amazement, a single tear rolled down the woman's dark face.

"I have a warning for you that is threefold," she whispered. She leaned forward so that her face was close to his. "Listen carefully to my words, Abraham Lincoln. Beware first the booth," she waved one long, lean finger in his face. "Second, beware the ford," she spoke slowly, deliberately, now holding two fingers in the air. "Finally," her dark eyes penetrated his as she uttered the third warning, and Abraham felt his heart begin to race in fear. "Beware the fourth month." Grabbing his hand, the oracle pleaded with him, "Heed these warnings, Abraham Lincoln, for your future holds much pain and much grief for many people."

Terrified by her words, Abraham shot up from the chair, knocking it over to the dirt floor of the stall. He yanked his hand away and jumped back from the table. "I do not understand these so-called warnings, madam!" he exclaimed. "You are a fraud, a sham. What a fool I was to waste my money on a soothsayer like you!" Snatching a penny from his vest pocket, he threw it on the table.

"Wait!" the fortune-teller cried. Snatching up the copper coin and turning it over in her hand, she examined the woman's head on one side, and the marking "one cent" on the reverse. "Even this coin calls out to me!" she shrieked. "Even it pronounces your fate! Take note of my words, Abraham!" With that, she began to laugh a terrible, frightening screeching laugh that caused goose bumps to break out all over Abraham's arms. Even as he darted from the booth and sprinted back down the alley, he could not escape the horrific sound of that woman's laughter. It was a sound that would haunt him forever.

* * *

Later that evening while Abraham stood on the top deck of the ship, he considered again the strange message the woman had given him. *Beware the ford,* he mused. *Ford, like fording a river? And beware the booth? What kind of booth? Why must I beware the month of April?* He shook his head in confusion. *These so-called warnings are ridiculous, and I am foolish for giving them another thought.*

Lincoln immediately turned his attention to other things. He watched as the ship's crew continued loading supplies for their journey down the Mississippi, and he admired the evening sky as the sunset sparkled in the rolling waters of the river. When the sun finally completed its descent into the Missouri horizon, Abraham walked down the steps to his cabin.

Stretched out on his bed as he waited for sleep to come, he again pondered the strange words spoken by the oracle. Comforting himself with the notion that she really was just a fraud, he felt himself drift off into a fitful sleep. Later that night, he awoke suddenly, his bedclothes soaked with perspiration and his muscles aching with tension. A thought came to him like a lightening bolt from the sky. He sat straight up in his bed.

In the lonesome quiet of the Mississippi River night, Abraham asked his question aloud in the darkness, "How did she know my name?"

* * *

The next morning, over a breakfast of tea and biscuits, Captain Richardson listened as Lincoln told him about the oracle's warnings.

"Ah, very interesting, Abraham," he said. "I do believe that there are those among us who have powers that can't be explained in human terms. For example, my great-great-great-grandmother was a pirate captain named Hannah Dunne. She sailed aboard her ship, *The Devil Ray*, looking for Indians to sell into slavery. She told a story about a Calusa Indian girl she'd captured who actually stopped a fierce hurricane with a handful of tobacco she threw from the crow's nest."

The captain sipped his tea, and then continued. "There are things in this world, Abraham, that don't make sense to our human brains, but that doesn't make them any less true."

"But this is foolish, isn't it?" Abraham asked, his eyes pleading. "It's just that there was something about the way she spoke. I can't get her words out of my mind." Abraham shook his head and chewed his biscuit thoughtfully.

"Well, you know that the Greeks believed in fortune-tellers. According to the story, there were three women who were called the Three Fates, and they decided how long someone would live. They could even see into the future. When a mortal was born, one of the Fates, Clotho, spun the thread of life. Another, Lachesis, measured the thread, and finally, Atropos cut the thread at the end of the life. Not even Zeus, king of the gods, had any power over them."

After pausing for a swallow of tea, Captain Richardson concluded, "Maybe the oracle's warnings are true, but maybe they are just the fancy of a strange woman's imagination. I wouldn't let them trouble me further. Come up on deck with me and breathe in some of this fine winter air! By this time tomorrow we'll be docked in Cape Girardeau!"

12

A Telltale Scar

Willie Hall sat on the lumpy cot, his back propped against the cold jailhouse wall. Through the bars on the small window, he could see the morning sunlight as it approached, but he was not cheered by the prospect of the brand-new day. "I don't think I can stand one more day behind these bars," he muttered, as he pulled a tattered blanket around his shoulders. His breakfast, a bowl of cold mush and a cup of tepid coffee, still waited for him on a stool in the corner of the cell. Willie had no stomach for it this morning. "Why does it have to be so gosh darn cold in this place?" he yelled to the guard. "A man could freeze to death in here! And when can I get a decent meal? I wouldn't feed this mess to dogs."

He kicked the stool over with the toe of his battered boot, and the dishes clattered to the floor.

"Shut up, Willie," the guard growled back at him. "What do you think this is? Your mama's kitchen?"

Willie pulled the thin blanket over his head, and curled his skinny body into a ball, trying to warm himself. He sat like that for a long time, thinking about the trouble that had brought him to this miserable prison, and wondering just what had gone wrong.

* * *

Using the seventy-five dollars from the sale of Isaiah, Willie had bought supplies and headed north, away from Hopkinsville, to the tiny town of Sparta, Illinois. "Don't need to stay in one place too long," Willie had told his men.

They found a little church just outside of town. Two of the gang had spotted the horses first, tied to hitching posts near the side of the building. "At least a dozen of them," Willie told his men, "and ripe for the picking." Tucking his father's worn Bible under his arm and donning his broad-brimmed hat, the black color matching his staid preacher's suit, Willie climbed the steps to the doors of the Methodist church. His gang knew what to do next and began going about their business as usual.

The service had not yet begun when Willie made his way down the center aisle, greeting the members with warm smiles and polite nods as he went. No one seemed to notice that the good preacher kept his right hand, poorly bandaged in grimy gauze, securely tucked in the pocket of his jacket. When he reached the altar at the front of the sanctuary, he turned to face the congregation. "Good morning, brothers and sisters! I am Preacher Hezekiah Hargiss, and I'm passing through your lovely town of Sparta on the way to visit my poor ailing mother in Cape Girardeau. What a pleasure it is to find such a warm and welcoming congregation to worship with on this cold winter's day!"

Like butterflies drawn to the first flower of spring, the people of the church crowded around the charismatic Preacher Hargiss. "We are such a small congregation that we do not have a regular minister," the elder of the church told him. "We truly ache for some real preaching from an educated man like yourself. Would you share the word of God with us this morning, Preacher?" And before they knew what was happening, Willie Hall, alias Preacher Hargiss, had launched into the longest, loudest, fire-and-brimstone sermon that any of those lifelong Methodists had ever heard.

"Do not store up for yourselves treasures on earth, where thieves break in and steal! No, no, no! Ladies and gentlemen, it is our responsibility to share with those who are poor, who are in need! Don't you agree?" Willie hollered his words, so that they echoed in the little building. The effect was dramatic, and the tiny congregation responded with a fervent, "Amen!"

He continued, his voice rising to the rafters. "If we see a brother in need, do we ignore him? Do we walk by and pretend we don't see his need? Or should we help him like the Good Samaritan who cared for the needs of a total stranger? Help him, I say! Help him!"

Again the congregation called out, "Amen!"

Willie could feel the excitement of the congregation growing as he preached earnestly and enthusiastically. Not for the first time, Willie wondered if maybe he hadn't been meant to be a preacher like his long-dead father. In any event, he was grateful to his mother for dragging him to church every Sunday. Not because he believed anything that the Sunday school teachers had taught him, however, but because he had listened well and had learned his Bible stories. He had enough sermon fodder in his brain to go on preaching like this forever.

According to his plan, Willie would distract the little congregation with his loud, boisterous preaching while his gang gathered the people's horses together and made off with them. Willie knew that by now every horse that had been tied at the church had disappeared. He smiled.

"Let us bow our heads for the benediction," Willie said sweetly. After a brief prayer, the service ended.

Standing at the back of the sanctuary, Willie greeted the worshippers one by one. They thanked him fervently for his preaching, and invited him to return whenever he was in their town. Willie smiled humbly, his eyes cast to the floor. "You all are much too kind," he replied modestly.

The confusion began as the people went to the side yard to reclaim their horses for the ride home. "They're gone!" one man yelled. "Every one of them is gone! We've been robbed! Some sorry thief took our horses!"

Willie quietly stole to the back door of the sanctuary, where his own horse waited for him just outside. Mounting quickly, Willie was gone in a flash.

"I hope they enjoyed their lesson on giving to the needy! Let's see if they can practice what *I* preach!" Willie laughed out loud as he headed straight to the meeting place, a cave near Thebes, a little village on the shores of the Mississippi River. A few of the local people knew of the hideout and called it the Devil's Den. It was meant as an insult, Willie knew, but he took it as a compliment. He grinned at their fear. He knew they'd never turn him in to the local sheriff because they were too frightened. Willie believed in getting revenge on those who betrayed him.

So, confident that he had made a clean getaway from the little Sparta Methodist Church, Willie rode straight to the corral where the stolen horses were being kept. "Just like clockwork!" He bragged to himself about the well-designed plan. "I've outsmarted every sheriff around. They'll never catch me again!"

Lost in his thoughts, Willie removed the bandages he had placed on his right thumb. The red, ragged H and T still looked raw, even after all these months. Down in Hopkinsville, just before he and his gang had run up on Isaiah, he'd been careless, and had actually robbed the sheriff's own church. That had been a big mistake. In his anger, the sheriff and some of his deputies had caught up with him after Willie's gang had stolen a dozen or so horses the same way he had in Sparta. He was lucky those townspeople didn't hang him on the spot. Instead, the sheriff himself had taken a knife and carved the sign for Horse Thief into his thumb, the HT that would never disappear.

While the people had waited for the circuit judge to arrive for his trial, his gang had busted him out of jail. Stealing horses is a hanging offense, he knew, but it was also a fast way to make a load of money. Willie had more greed than brains.

Now, dismounting at his hideout, he left his horse with the others in the corral and sauntered smugly into the cave, ready to celebrate with his men. With over an hour's head start, he knew his gang would already be well into their beer and whiskey by now, reveling over their latest success. An unwelcome surprise awaited him.

His arrogance and overconfidence proved to be his downfall, for had he been more cautious, he might have realized that his perfect plan had gone awry. First he might have noticed the silence. The men should have been laughing, joking, and generally carrying on, but the cave was eerily quiet. Then, there was the darkness. As he strode deeper into the cave, he should have seen the torches that lit the inner room where the gang usually holed up. There was only blackness ahead. Then suddenly, the Sparta sheriff and his deputies had surrounded him, their guns drawn and their fingers itching to shoot the infamous horse thief, Willie Hall.

* * *

Now, locked up in the jail in Cape Girardeau where the sheriff had deposited him, Willie sat alone in his cell. He realized, with irony, that the lookout he insisted be posted night and day must have seen the posse coming, and had warned the men in time for them to make their escape. He was the only one caught, and he was the only one certain to hang for this crime.

Now, he had only one hope to escape the noose: an inexperienced country lawyer his mother had hired to defend him, a brand-spanking-new attorney from Springfield by the name of Abraham Lincoln.

13

The Spurious Preacher

"Lawyer's here, Willie," the guard snarled as he unlocked the cell door for Abraham to enter. Willie looked at his attorney, studied him up and down, and rolled his eyes in disgust. He instantly decided that this man was too young, too green, to protect him from the hangman. *If he's going to be my lawyer*, Willie thought, *I might as well start filling out my last will and testament right now.*

"Hello, Willie," Lincoln began, and held out his right hand to his client. Without meeting Lincoln's eyes, Willie grunted a greeting, but kept his scarred hand securely hidden in his pocket. Abraham ignored the slight, and continued. "Your mother sent me here to help you. She's a fine woman, and I think very highly of her. Even though I don't cotton to horse thieves, I'm willing to try to get you a fair trial, for her sake. Now, why don't you tell me what happened?" Lincoln pulled the stool closer to the cot, and sat down, patiently waiting for his client to begin.

Resignedly, Willie told his story to his lawyer. Figuring he had nothing to lose, he even told him the truth instead of trying to make up lies or excuses for his actions. Lincoln showed no emotion but just listened intently. Willie soon found that he enjoyed bragging about his exploits to this young lawyer, and so he confessed everything, even some crimes he'd committed but never been charged with.

"There was one poor fellow, a slave named Isaiah, who I found one night hiding out with his sister in the woods. They were trying to get to the North. Runaways, you know." Willie smirked at the memory. "Stupid boy," he said. "I told him I'd sell him to a plantation owner down there near Hopkinsville for one hundred dollars, leave him there for a week or so, and then come steal him back. I promised to split the money with him." Willie snorted. "The fool believed me. I sold him all right." Then, with a sly wink he added, "Would you believe I just plain forgot to go steal him back? Reckon he's still there on the plantation, waiting for old Willie to come rescue him. Going to have a long wait now, isn't he?" Suddenly serious again, Willie got up from the cot, and walked over to the window. Grabbing hold of the bars that covered the small opening, he spoke with his back to the lawyer.

"What I can't figure out," Willie said, shaking his head, "is how they caught me. We'd used this same plan over and over. Except for that one time at the sheriff's church, it worked perfectly. What went wrong?"

"I can tell you that," Lincoln replied, stretching out his long legs on the cot. "When you started your preaching in that little church in Sparta, you thought all of the church members were already inside the building. Your men set about their work, but they were being watched. A certain man, a man named Buddy Lee, had been caring for his sick wife that morning, and was late for the service. He saw what your men were doing and went to the sheriff in Sparta for help." Lincoln paused for a moment, letting his words sink in.

"The sheriff, his deputies, and Mister Lee arrived back at the church in time to see you ride away at full gallop, and they figured you were heading back to your hideout to meet up with your men. You were so all-fired sure that your plan had worked that you never looked back to see if you were being followed." Willie moaned at this point, realizing what a fool he'd been.

Abraham went on, "In those Sunday school classes your mother took you to each week, did you ever hear the Bible verse, 'Pride goes before destruction, a haughty spirit before a fall'? Well, Willie, your greed and pride put you in this cell. The only one who's innocent here is your ma, and I'm here for her sake, not yours." Abraham got up to leave, signaling for the guard to come unlock the door. He barely heard Willie's next words.

"I don't want to die, Mr. Lincoln," Willie whispered. "Can you help me?"

"I'll see what I can do, Willie," was all Abraham said and he walked out of the cell.

* * *

Days passed slowly for Willie. He spent his time pacing back and forth across the tiny room, wrapped in blankets, trying to stay warm. During the week, two or three guards were always on duty, sitting outside the cell in a snug little room that had its own wood stove. It made Willie colder just looking at it. Today there was only one guard there, and he looked none too happy. *Must be Sunday. Not much excitement around here today so they sent all the other guards home.* Willie mused, *Everybody else will be at church or home in bed. This one's mad 'cause he missed Sunday dinner.* Willie grinned wickedly. *Too bad for him!*

He counted off the days in his mind, and realized that he'd been in this prison nearly a month. Today being Sunday, a local preacher would come to have a word with the prisoners. He would read the Bible and then spend some time in prayer with them, pondering their sins and encouraging them to repent. Even though he was told that there was only one prisoner in the Cape Girardeau jail today, a useless horse thief named Willie Hall, the preacher would not be dissuaded from his mission. A lone jailer was reluctantly pulled from his Sunday supper to let him in to see Willie.

"Fool preacher," he muttered as he opened the jailhouse door for the stocky, red-faced man, "thinking anybody can save Willie Hall. He's nothing but a worthless excuse for a human being." The jailer noted that he'd never seen this preacher before but then, he didn't spend too many Sunday mornings darkening the doorways of churches.

"Thank you, sir," the friendly preacher tipped his hat and smiled as he came through the open door. "I'm sorry to take you away from your dinner, but every soul is important to God."

"Let's just get this over with," the jailer mumbled darkly as he led the preacher down the stone hallway to the only occupied cell in the building.

"All by yourself today, I see," the preacher remarked jovially, as he followed his escort. He looked into each empty cell as he walked, making sure the coast was clear.

"Yes, everybody else is at home enjoying fried chicken and biscuits, and here I am. . . ." His words were cut short as the handle of the preacher's pistol hit him squarely in the back of the skull. Soundlessly, he crumbled to the floor. His attacker relieved him of the keys to the cells.

"Willie, where are you?" the preacher called out. "It's Davey. I'm here to get you out!"

Willie jumped to his feet and threw his arms through the bars of his cell. "Over here, Davey!" he hollered. "Boy, am I glad to see you! I thought you'd all just leave me here to hang. Should've known you'd come back for me."

Davey stuck the large skeleton key into the lock, and swung the cell door wide for Willie. They ran down the hall, stopping briefly to check on the guard who was still sprawled unconscious on the floor. "Help me tie him up," Willie said. "He's not going to wake up for quite a while, but the longer we can keep him quiet, the further away we can get from the sheriff's posse." They dragged the guard into a nearby cell, tied him with rope, and stuffed a rag in his mouth. Grinning at Davey, Willie commented, "That was quite a lick you put on him!"

Davey smiled at his boss. "C'mon! Let's get out of here. That man was already madder than a hornet in a pickle barrel. He must have missed his Sunday supper because of me."

Willie turned and looked at Davey. "Madder than a what?" he

asked, laughing.

"Just something my ma used to say," Davey replied sheepishly. "One thing's for sure, though. When he wakes up with that headache I just gave him, he's going to be seeing red, and we need to be as far away as we can get!"

Davey donned his preacher hat and put his gun back in its hiding place under his jacket. "Wait here and I'll bring the horses around." As calmly as any preacher enjoying a lovely Sunday afternoon, Davey strolled down the narrow walk and around to the back of the jail. Two horses were tied up, waiting. Davey led them back around to the front and handed the reins of one to Willie. The men mounted the horses, and then sauntered serenely down the main thoroughfare of Cape Girardeau, heading to the south and east, back toward Kentucky. It must have seemed to the casual observer that the pair didn't have a worry in the world.

* * *

Abraham scrubbed his broad hand across his furrowed brow. His shoulders ached with tension and his eyes burned from overuse. He'd been working on Willie's case for days, spending hour after hour searching through dusty law books, looking for a way to defend his client in court. His quest had turned up nothing, and on this cold Monday morning the young lawyer was tired and discouraged.

"You're wasting your time and energy on this one," his friend Clayton Collins had said when he arrived at his office to find Abraham already there, up to his elbows in legal documents. Clayton, an old family friend, had allowed Abraham complete access to his firm's extensive law library, and gratefully, he had taken full advantage.

Seeing his young friend's frustration, Clayton patted him on the arm. "You'll think of something," the older man had told Lincoln, trying to assure him. "Look how you took care of that case in Springfield, getting that man out of a murder charge, claiming self- defense." Clayton's thick gray mustache turned up in a mischievous grin. "That man killed somebody by hitting him over the head with a chair, and you got the jury to believe he was just protecting himself." Clayton shook his bushy white head. "That was some pretty fancy dancing you did there, Abraham."

"That man really did strike out in self-defense, Clayton," Lincoln replied grimly. "Willie, on the other hand, really did steal those horses."

"Exactly!" Clayton said, raising his stocky body from his chair. He continued speaking, his thick arms gesturing as if he were addressing a jury. "He's guilty, no doubt about it. He has a right to a good defense in court, and you're going to give it to him. But," he continued seriously, peering over the top of his spectacles, "you can't expect to work miracles. Do the best you can, Abraham."

Lincoln stood up and walked to the window. Through the smudged glass, he could see the busy street of Cape Girardeau two stories below. Thinking of Miriam Hall, his heart sank. "She's counting on me, Clayton, and there's very little that I can do to save her son's life. What will I tell her?"

"Abraham," Clayton said gently, "Willie broke the law. The punishment for stealing horses in this state is hanging. There's not much you can do!" Clayton extended his hands in desperation, trying to reassure his young friend.

Their conversation was interrupted by the arrival of a messenger at the office door. "Are you Abraham Lincoln?" the man asked. When Abraham nodded his head, the man shoved a small greasy paper in his hand, tipped his hat, and left. Lincoln unfolded the note and began to read.

"What is it?" Clayton asked, trying to decipher Abraham's incredulous expression. "What's happened?"

Abraham's face had turned as white as old bones blanching in the desert sun. Moving slowly to the desk, he dropped heavily into his chair. Wearily laying his head in his hands, Abraham sighed deeply. "This message is from the sheriff's office. He's escaped, Clayton. Yesterday afternoon, Willie Hall escaped from the Cape Girardeau jail."

14

Two Together

Daybreak the next morning found the Cherokee camp covered in deep drifts of snow, but the skies had changed from dull gray to an icy winter blue. John had crawled under the wagon with his grandfather late last night, hoping to help warm him in the terrible storm. He woke now to the frightening sound of Gray Hawk's coughing.

"Stay here, Grandfather, while I find some water for you. Let me cover you with my blanket. I'll be back quickly." John tucked his blanket around Gray Hawk's shoulders, and crawled out into the weak light of early morning. He was surprised to find Captain Cannon walking among the wagons, talking to the Indians, and inquiring about the sick.

"How is your grandfather today, John?" he asked. The boy could see that concern for the people in his care had already carved deep creases in the captain's face. His eyes were bloodshot and tired, further evidence of his distress.

"This weather is not good for him, Captain," John answered politely. "His cough is much worse this morning, and though he speaks of being cold, his forehead burns with fever. I do not know how to help him."

"He is a great leader for your people. They rely on his strength and encouragement." Captain Cannon rubbed his hand over his whiskers, deep in thought. "If I bring my horse to him, do you think we could help him ride?"

"Where would we take him?" John asked worriedly. "He will not leave The People."

"The owners of this farm have a large house just over the hill. Perhaps they would allow Gray Hawk to stay there, out of this cold, until he's better." Captain Cannon placed his hand on John's shoulder. "The People need him, John, and so do you. I will do whatever I can to help him get well."

Gratitude shone from John's eyes as he looked up into the captain's face. "I would be so thankful, Captain Cannon. If they will allow me to, I will stay with Grandfather so that he will not be a burden to them."

"Let me see what can be arranged, John. I'll return as quickly as I can." Captain Cannon smiled at the boy, and then trudged away through the drifts toward the other side of the pasture. For the first time in weeks, John's heart was filled with hope.

Several hours later, Captain Cannon returned, leading his horse around the deepest drifts to where John stood waiting with his grandfather. Gray Hawk was sitting on a blanket in the snow, resting against the rear wheel of the wagon. "John," Captain Cannon said, "help me get him on the horse."

Though weakened by his illness, Gray Hawk found the strength to protest. "Do not offer me help when you leave others of my people behind who are also in need. I will not go if they cannot come as well."

John became indignant with his grandfather, but Captain Cannon spoke gently to the old man. "I suspected that you might feel this way, Gray Hawk. You are truly a great leader. Do not be alarmed, for I have made arrangements for them as well.

"The owners of this farm have consented to allow us to use their barn as a hospital for the very ill," he continued. "As soon as we have taken care of your needs, I will send my soldiers to do the same for those among The People who are sick. They will be well-cared for."

Upon hearing Captain Cannon's words, Gray Hawk grunted

his approval and struggled to his feet. With John's help, he climbed awkwardly astride the captain's horse. Barely able to hold his head erect, he leaned heavily on John, who sat behind him on the sturdy mare. John wrapped his arms firmly around his grandfather to steady him. Captain Cannon took the reins and slowly walked his horse around the deepest drifts and up the hill to the main house.

A wonderful surprise awaited Gray Hawk and John at the top of the little knoll. For as soon as they spotted the two riders led by Captain Cannon, Charles and Susannah Thompson ran to the front door, opening it wide to welcome their friends. "Gray Hawk! John!" Susannah cried joyously. "It's so wonderful to see you again!" Then, eyeing the older man's obvious discomfort, she began to bark orders at the men. "Charles, quickly help the captain get Gray Hawk into the back bedroom. John, there's a pot of soup warming on the stove. Put some in a bowl and bring it to me. Hurry!"

At Susannah's direction, Gray Hawk was laid in a soft bed piled high with quilts and pillows. A fire was started in the small stove to warm the room, and a kerosene lantern provided light for Susannah to examine her patient. Feeling his forehead, she shook her head worriedly. "I'll need some cool, fresh water, some clean rags, and extra blankets. Go quickly, Charles."

Gray Hawk's voice was weak as he spoke to the young woman. "Thank you, Susannah, for your concern, but please go see to my people. They are in great need. I will be fine now that I am out of the cold wind and snow." Gray Hawk coughed violently, and Susannah propped more pillows behind his head. She offered him some cool water, which he sipped gratefully. Finally, he could speak again, his words full of emotion, "My heart is like *unestalun*, like ice, filled with worry for The People. I do not know what is to become of them." John came into the room carrying a large bowl, its contents steaming and fragrant.

"First, let me take care of you, Gray Hawk," Susannah replied. "Then, I promise I will check on the others. Captain Cannon has sent a soldier into the town to bring the doctor for you and your people." Dipping a large spoon into the bowl, she fed the broth to Gray Hawk. "You must try to eat just a little. This soup will help strengthen you." After a few sips, the old man was exhausted and laid his head on the cool white pillow.

"I will rest now," he said wearily, and closed his eyes. Soon, to John's great relief, his grandfather was softly snoring.

Susannah took the rags that John had brought, soaked one in the cool water, and placed it gently on Gray Hawk's forehead. Covering him with still another quilt, she whispered, "Stay here with your grandfather, John. Resting in a nice warm bed may be the best medicine for him right now."

She patted John's hand reassuringly. "I will go see about the others in the barn. Call me if there is anything that you need." Smiling at her young friend, Susannah slipped out the door, closing it gently behind her.

* * *

Annie woke from a fitful sleep. She'd been dreaming about Isaiah, his cries so loud that she thought his voice was real. In her dream she'd seen him on a plantation, dressed in rags and freezing in the snow. He called her name over and over again, causing tears to run down her cheeks. *Where are you, Isaiah?* She cried, burying her head in her pillow.

Suddenly a noise in the room above startled her. She was accustomed to the everyday sounds that Miss Susannah's soft step made, but these noises were made by men's boots. Charles was making some of the footsteps, she was certain, but there was someone else as well. She heard voices, too, that were strange and unfamiliar. They were men's voices, she realized, and they were coming through the ceiling to her little hiding place beneath the kitchen. Frightened and unsure as to what she should do, Annie hid herself behind the bins of potatoes.

"Annie? Don't be afraid." Miss Susannah's voice was soothing, and the girl came out from her hiding place. "There you are! We have some unexpected guests in the house. Two of our

87

Cherokee friends, Gray Hawk and his grandson John, will be staying with us for awhile. Gray Hawk is very sick and needs my attention." Susannah moved to the little stove and put a log into the fire. The room was instantly brighter and warmer.

"Please be very quiet. If John and Gray Hawk knew our secret they would be in danger just as we are. You must not be discovered."

Annie nodded, and Miss Susannah moved toward the little staircase. "I think that the soup we made together yesterday is going to prove to be a blessing to many of the Cherokee. Thank you for your help, Annie. I will bring some food down to you shortly." Susannah quickly climbed the stairs back to the kitchen. Annie heard the little panel door at the top of the stairs slide shut, leaving her alone again with nothing but her fear for company.

Later that day while Gray Hawk slept, John decided that he could contain his own hunger no longer. He did not want to leave his grandfather's side for even a second, but he smelled Miss Susannah's soup simmering on the stove, and his stomach voiced its impatience with loud grumbling and gurgling. Leaning over the bed, John whispered softly so that he wouldn't disturb Gray Hawk's sleep. "I'll be right back, Grandfather." Touching the old man's forehead, he could tell that the fever was better. Encouraged, John quietly shuffled from the room and headed for the kitchen.

As he walked through the main sitting room, John's attention was captured by an object hanging on a brass hook just above the mantle of the fireplace. He smiled as he recognized the eagle feather that Gray Hawk had given as a gift of gratitude to the Thompsons on that terrible day so many months ago. "What good friends you have proven yourselves to be," he whispered, thinking how fortunate he and his grandfather were to have found Susannah and Charles on this sad journey.

Moving quickly to the kitchen, John took a bowl from the table and ladled soup into it. Tearing a large chunk of bread from a freshly baked loaf, he turned to hurry back to Gray Hawk, but paused when a thought crossed his mind. *Perhaps Grandfather will want some water,* he considered, and he looked about the cluttered kitchen for a cup. Several chipped pottery cups were hanging on hooks on the opposite side of the room. Taking one down from its hook, John stopped to study the paneled wall. *There's something strange about this wall,* John mused. *It seems crooked, somehow, or maybe it's just not level.* He stepped away to get a better look.

Grandfather's voice interrupted the boy's thoughts. "John? John?" Gray Hawk called weakly. "Could I have some water please?"

"I'll be right there, Grandfather!" John exclaimed, and in that instant all thoughts about the strange wall flew from his mind.

The afternoon slowly passed. Grandfather slept for an hour at a time, waking only to ask John for water. In between times, John occupied himself by reading old Cherokee newspapers that the Thompsons had kept in bundles in the corner of the room. He smiled as he read, thinking about the many times he had read these same papers to his grandfather. Presently, exhausted by worry and drowsy from reading, he fell asleep in the old cane rocking chair where he'd been keeping watch.

Sunset was coloring the Kentucky sky with winter streaks of amber and scarlet when John finally awoke. He stood up and shook his head to clear his brain of sleepy cobwebs. The house was eerily silent. "The Thompsons must still be outside tending to The People," he mumbled, and then rubbing his eyes, John leaned over the bed to get a closer look at his grandfather. The old man was sleeping comfortably. "No coughing," he said, and then touching Gray Hawk's forehead, "no fever, either." Rising stiffly from the chair, John limped into the kitchen once more to get fresh water, for he knew that his grandfather would soon be asking for some.

When John went to dip some water from the wooden bucket Miss Susannah had in the kitchen, he realized that it was nearly dry. Wrapping a warm quilt around his shoulders and grabbing the bucket, the boy limped to the kitchen door. Steeling himself against the cold, he opened the door and headed out into the cold dusk, intent upon drawing some fresh water for Grandfather. It was a brief walk to the well, but John's leg made moving in the deep drifts very difficult. The return trip was made even more challenging by the heavy bucket of water sloshing around his legs. The comforting heat of the cozy kitchen was his well-earned reward, and he burst in the door, happy at last to be warm.

* * *

Shut away in the cellar room, Annie could barely tolerate her confinement. The small space was warm and dry with the little stove glowing comfortingly, but still she was very lonely. "Surely Miss Susannah needs somebody in the kitchen to help prepare food for all those poor, sick people," Annie said aloud, shattering the silence that had saturated every inch of her hiding place. "I haven't heard any more strange voices or footsteps in hours. I could go upstairs to the kitchen, chop some vegetables, and heat some broth." She paused thoughtfully for a minute before continuing. "I'll keep the door open at the top of the stairs, just in case someone comes in." With her mind made up, she resolutely climbed the stairs, pausing at the top to listen through the door for any sound on the other side. Hearing nothing, Annie pulled the latch, and slid the door into the recess in the wall.

She stood with her back to the door, busily chopping potatoes and turnips at the scarred wooden table in the middle of the kitchen. All at once the back door burst open, and in came a gush of cold winter wind, accompanied by a startled-looking Cherokee boy bearing a water bucket. The young slave girl and the Indian boy both jumped in alarm. Annie's paring knife clattered to the floor while John's bucket splashed water everywhere.

"Who are you?" John cried. Annie started to back toward the cellar door, but John grabbed her wrist, halting her retreat.

"Oh, dear," murmured Miss Susannah who had come through

the door just in time to witness the commotion. "John, you may let go of Annie. She is a guest here, just as you are." John released his grip, but still eyed the stranger suspiciously. "Annie," Miss Susannah continued, "this is John. He is the son of Gray Hawk, a noble leader of the Cherokee, and our friend. Gray Hawk is very ill, and he and John will be staying with us until he is well enough to travel again."

"I'm sorry, Miss Susannah," Annie stammered. "I know that I'm not supposed to be up here, but I was so lonely down in the cellar, and I thought that I could help chop vegetables for you." Motioning at the vegetables she'd been preparing, Annie said weakly, "I left the door open, so that I'd be able to run downstairs if anyone came. I guess I was wrong about that." The girl's eyes filled with tears.

"It's all right, Annie. I shouldn't have left you alone so long." Miss Susannah put her arm around the girl's shoulder. "You must be terribly worried about your brother. I know that you were just trying to help."

"John, go check on your grandfather, and then come back here," Miss Susannah said. "Annie and I will explain everything."

John gave Miss Susannah a puzzled look, but then hurriedly limped through the sitting room and down the hall to Gray Hawk's room. He found his grandfather still sleeping comfortably. When he got back to the kitchen, Annie and Miss Susannah had disappeared, but the strange door in the paneled wall was ajar.

"John, we're down here," Miss Susannah called softly. "Come down the stairs slowly. I'm holding the light for you."

Looking down through the small door, John could indeed see a tiny staircase with a light softly glowing at the bottom. He could just make out Miss Susannah's face in the dimness. Carefully, he climbed through the opening in the wall, and made his way down the stairs.

Once at the bottom, he studied the room with interest. He took in the cots with pillows and blankets along the wall, the small stove that provided warmth, and the tiny hidden door at the end of the room. "A secret room!" he exclaimed with delight. "No one would even know that it was here!"

"Unless the person who's supposed to be hiding lets the secret out," Annie mumbled dismally. She plopped herself down on the cot, pulled her legs to her chest, and hid her face in her hands.

Miss Susannah went over to Annie and sat down next to her. Rubbing her back comfortingly, she began to tell John the story of Annie and Isaiah. John remained silent, listening intently to the tale Miss Susannah told.

When she got to the part where Isaiah allowed himself to be sold back into slavery, however, John could contain himself no longer. "But that was so brave!" he exclaimed admiringly. "I don't know if I'd ever have the courage to do that."

Annie perked up at his words. "Really, John? Really? You think that Isaiah was brave?" she asked hopefully.

"Of course, Annie," John replied. He pulled a stool close to the cot and leaned toward the girl, his eyes meeting hers. He spoke earnestly. "It may not have been very smart, but it took lots of courage. I'd be very proud if I had a brother who would face danger like that for me."

For the first time all day, Annie found herself smiling. And by the time Miss Susannah had finished the story, Annie knew that she and Isaiah had found a new friend in this Cherokee boy named John.

15
Just Like Gideon

"Annie, it looks like you'll be staying with us for a few more days," Mr. Charles announced that night after supper. He and Miss Susannah had come to Annie's room to bring her some food and to tell her the news. "This snow has made the roads impassable for horses or wagons, and you'll just need to wait here until the weather improves."

Annie beamed with delight. Although she was eager to see her parents and little Jacob again, she welcomed the delay. She feared that the Thompsons had to make her travel on to the North without Isaiah. She could endanger Mr. Charles and Miss Susannah if she stayed too long, because someone might see her. Now that the snow had come, she would have a few extra days to try to devise a plan to rescue her brother. She heard her mother's voice from long ago quietly speaking in her heart.

"Remember, Annie," Mama would say. "The Bible teaches us that 'in all things God works for the good of those who love him.'" *You're right again, Mama!* Annie thought happily. *Surely Mr. Charles will figure out a way to get Isaiah free!*

"Now Annie, I know this Stuart Cooper that Isaiah has been sold to. His farm is just a few miles from here, down the Hopkinsville Road. I'm afraid that there's little we can do to help your brother. Cooper is a very difficult man." Charles paused, choosing his next words carefully. "I will contact some of my

93

abolitionist friends tomorrow to see if they can help me raise the money we'd need to buy Isaiah from him, but I'm not hopeful. You'd better resign yourself to going on without him." Charles saw the crestfallen expression on the girl's face and tried to comfort her. "Don't give up hope, Annie!"

Later that evening while Miss Susannah sat with Gray Hawk, John came down the secret staircase to visit Annie. Mr. Charles had told him about the plan to buy Isaiah's freedom from Stuart Cooper, and John knew that Annie would be worried about her brother. He found her sitting on her cot in the warm glow of the little stove. Falling tears had marked the girl's face with moist tracks, but she attempted a thin smile when she saw her friend.

"I know how worried you must be about Isaiah, Annie," John said gently. "I thought maybe you'd like some company. I brought a Cherokee game with me that I thought might help distract you for a little while. Would you like to play?" Taking handfuls of sticks from a pouch tied at his waste, John made two large piles. "Here, I'll show you how. There are fifty-one sticks altogether. All you have to do is guess whether your pile has an even or odd amount." John smiled at her. "It's harder than you think. I beat Grandfather every time we play!"

Annie looked down at the small pile in front of her. She didn't feel much like playing, but John had been very thoughtful to come see her, and she did not want to hurt his feelings. After all, she knew how worried he must be about his grandfather, and yet he came to see her, hoping to cheer her up.

"I'll guess odd," she said blandly.

"I think you're wrong, Annie, and I brought something to make this game a little more interesting." From his pouch John pulled a handful of freshly baked sugar cookies, no doubt taken from Miss Susannah's kitchen without her knowledge. He broke them into pieces, and divided them between himself and Annie. "We'll each put one piece in the middle and whoever wins the round gets the cookie pieces."

Annie put a large piece of cookie in the middle of the blanket, and then counted her sticks. John was right; she had thirty-two sticks in her pile.

Grinning broadly, John snatched up the two cookie pieces and began to distribute the sticks for another round. John's good cheer was contagious, and Annie began to feel a little better.

"I'm glad you're here, John," she smiled wanly. "I'm so worried about Isaiah, and there's nothing that I can do." She wrung her hands in frustration. "I wish I had money. I'd go buy him back right now."

"Maybe there's another way, Annie," John said slowly. "Perhaps we could help him escape."

Annie looked at him questioningly. "Escape? How would we do that?" she asked. The idea had already occurred to her, but she knew that she could never rescue Isaiah alone. Maybe with John's help, she could free her brother.

"Odd!" John said as Annie placed a handful of sticks in front of him. His pile of cookie pieces was steadily growing, while Annie's was down to crumbs. "I don't know, Annie, but there's got to be a way." He paused to count his sticks. "Twenty-nine! I win!" he exclaimed as he swept his hand across the blanket and collected his sugary prize. Sitting with his back resting against the cool wall, John chewed thoughtfully on one of the cookie pieces. He handed a large piece to Annie.

After a few moments, the boy spoke. "I remember a story from the Bible that Miss Susannah told us. It was about a man who defeated an entire army with just a few men and some trumpets. Now, what was his name?" His voice trailed off as he tried to recall the character from the story.

"Gideon!" Annie exclaimed enthusiastically. "I know that story!" She settled herself comfortably on the blanket, took another cookie, and began to tell the tale her mother had told her long ago.

"The Lord wanted to give his children, the Israelites, the land of Midian. He chose Gideon to be their leader. Now, Gideon had lots of men ready to fight, but the Lord didn't want that. He said that he didn't want the Israelites to brag about winning the battle themselves; He wanted them to know that they won only because their God helped them."

Annie paused, thinking. She wanted to get the story right for John. "So, God told Gideon to tell all his soldiers that if any of them were trembling with fear at the thought of fighting in this battle, they could go back. Lots and lots of them turned away, but there were still too many.

"So then God told Gideon to take the rest of the army down to the water. All the men were supposed to get a drink. Some got down on their knees to drink, while others lapped water from their hands. God wanted the men who lapped water to stay with Gideon. The ones who knelt down were sent home."

Annie was a good storyteller, and John was enthralled. "Go on," he said. "What happened next?"

"Gideon and his small group of men went down to attack the much larger army of the Midianites. He divided the men into three companies, and armed them only with trumpets and empty jars."

"That's it?" John asked incredulously. "How could anyone win a battle with no weapons?"

"That's the point of the story, John," Annie explained patiently. "God wanted the people to know that He gave them the victory. They didn't do it themselves." Shifting her legs under her, she continued with her story.

"Gideon and his men surrounded the enemy camp in the middle of the night. At Gideon's signal, they blew their trumpets and broke the jars. When the Midianites heard all the commotion, they must have thought that they were completely outnumbered. Anyway, they all ran away, and Gideon and his men won the battle." Finished with her tale, Annie bit into another cookie, while John sat quietly opposite her, deep in thought.

"We can do that, Annie," he said quietly. "We can create a

diversion, just like Gideon did with the trumpets and jars." Warming to the idea, John's eyes sparkled with excitement.

"John, I know you mean well, but we could never do anything like that," Annie said seriously. "There are just two of us, and Gideon had three hundred men! We'd get caught for sure, and end up causing trouble for Mr. Charles and Miss Susannah." Annie hugged her legs close to her chest and rested her chin on her knees.

"It's just an idea, Annie," he shrugged his shoulders. "Let me think about it, and maybe I can come up with a plan."

Thoughtfully, John pulled his flute from his belt and softly began to play. Annie was enchanted by the beauty of the simple melody. "Please, John," she begged, "can you teach me to play like that?"

John smiled. "I could try, Annie. My father taught me. He even made this flute for me. I'll never forget," he said quietly. "It was the summer before he died. Even though I was very little, he took me through the woods to a patch of cane growing tall in the sun. He selected just the right piece, and cut it with his knife." John's eyes had a faraway look, as if he were reliving the scene all over again. "He thanked the cane for giving itself to him, and then cut this piece."

He handed the flute to Annie, who gently turned it over in her hands to examine it closely. The flute was a burnished gold color, and had been worn smooth by the constant rubbing of John's hands.

"For days he worked on the cane, hollowing it exactly and smoothing any rough edges. Then, one afternoon, he carefully carved the holes that would make the music. I was so excited and so proud!" John took the flute from Annie's hands and rubbed it affectionately. "It's the one thing my father gave me that I will always treasure."

"Could you make one for me?" Annie asked softly, realizing that this was a great favor to ask of her new friend.

"I will try," he replied, relieved to see a glimmer of joy in his friend's eyes. Getting up to return to his grandfather's bedside,

John turned to Annie. "Don't lose hope. Your path and mine have become intertwined for a reason that only the Great Spirit knows. We will help each other." With a final smile, John limped up the stairs. By the time he reached the top, Annie was asleep.

16

Hihinalii

"You must take care of The People, John. I cannot tend to them now, and they need your help." Gray Hawk stopped speaking, his thin body wracked momentarily by a fit of coughing. John was dismayed; Grandfather had seemed so much better yesterday. His fever had seemed to disappear, and he hardly coughed at all. But this morning Gray Hawk was worse than when they arrived at the Thompson farm. After a sip of water, he spoke again. "Charles said that there are many sick, and he has taken the worst to his barn to provide them with some shelter. Go see if you can help them, John."

The boy studied his grandfather in the morning light. After a night filled with coughing and fever, the old man looked weary and frail. John did not want to leave Gray Hawk's side, but the young man did what he was told and struggled through the deep drifts to the barn.

John heard the terrible coughing before he got to the barn door. Coming from deep within lungs that were congested and diseased, the hacking sound was both sickening and terrifying. He knew that those inside were very seriously ill, and he had no medicine to help them. He entered the barn quietly, shocked to see the number of people contained there. There were old men and women curled on cots and covered with tattered blankets. Young children were cocooned in quilts like small, battered butterflies laying helter-skelter on the dirt floor. The smell of sickness permeated the air, and bile rose in John's throat.

Walking softly over to a group of the little children, John recognized Singing Brook, the tiny girl who had loved the story of the red bird. He smiled down at her, and she smiled back weakly. Her face was flushed with fever, and she coughed until John's throat ached in sympathy. Kneeling down, he asked her, "Singing Brook, would you like to hear a song?" She nodded her head feebly, and John pulled his flute from his belt. Placing the well-loved instrument to his lips, he prayed that this music would somehow bring comfort to The People, just as it had for generations.

He played softly at first, not wanting to disturb those in the barn who had found sweet relief from their illness in a brief period of sleep. But soon he saw that all of The People, young and old alike, were listening intently to the familiar songs that he played. Smiles lit faces that had not felt happiness for many days.

John shuffled from patient to patient, pausing by each one, to smile and play a short tune. Up and down the aisles of sickbeds he played, until he came to the darkest corner of the barn where old barrels and wooden crates had been piled to make room for the patients. One small keg in particular caught his attention. It was marked GUNPOWDER, and John's face exploded into a huge grin. "Now we have a plan!" he said softly, and putting the flute to his lips, he played a very happy tune.

* * *

It was late afternoon when the Thompsons heard the dreadful news. With grim faces, Charles and Susannah crept silently down the winding staircase to Annie's room. They found her sitting on her cot, playing the Cherokee stick game that John had taught her the night before. Smiling, Annie looked up when she heard their footsteps. "It's a difficult game," she said, "but I'm improving. I can't figure out how John counts these sticks so quickly!" When she noticed the dismal expressions on the faces of her friends, Annie asked worriedly, "What's wrong? Has something happened to Isaiah?"

"It's not Isaiah, honey," Miss Susannah said softly. Drawing Annie close, she sat beside her on the bed. "We've gotten some troubling news about your parents."

Annie sucked in her breath. Trembling all over, she looked first at Miss Susannah and then at Mr. Charles. "Tell me," she whispered, tears slowly gathering in her dark eyes.

"Annie, some friends of mine, abolitionist friends, told me about a certain Mr. Jones who was stopped by slave catchers on his way to the North. Apparently, Mr. Jones was transporting a man, a woman, and a little boy named Jacob in the false bottom of his wagon. Mr. Jones was beaten severely by the slave catchers and left to die in the woods in northern Alabama." Charles looked at Annie and saw tears running down her face and dropping onto her folded hands. Her shoulders were shaking with grief, and Charles felt his heart break for this poor, frightened girl.

"We're not sure what happened to the family in the wagon, but we can assume that the slave catchers took them back to the plantation they came from. That's the way those horrible men earn their living." He paused, letting his words sink in. "Your parents didn't complete their journey to freedom, Annie. I'm so sorry."

Annie sobbed and threw her arms around Miss Susannah's neck. "Poor Mama! Poor Papa! And Jacob! What will happen to Jacob?" She cried and cried for what seemed like hours. Even after she had shed all of her tears, Miss Susannah held her tightly, rocking her gently just as Annie's mother had rocked her long, long ago.

Mr. Charles found John sitting by Gray Hawk's bedside, as usual. He told the boy what had happened to Annie's family. "I'll sit with your grandfather while he sleeps," Charles spoke in hushed words so as not to disturb the old man. "You need to go talk to Annie. It might make her feel better to talk things over with a friend near her own age. I will call for you if Gray Hawk needs anything."

John nodded and tenderly patted his grandfather's silvery gray head. "I'll be back soon," he whispered. The old man grunted in his sleep but did not open his eyes.

Mr. Charles made himself comfortable in the chair, crossing his long legs and opening one of the old Cherokee newspapers. "Go on," Charles urged John, looking at him over the top of the page, "I'll take good care of him."

When Miss Susannah heard John's distinctive footsteps on the stairs, she rose from the cot where she'd been trying to console Annie. The girl was quiet now, lying at the foot of the little bed. The despair in her eyes troubled Susannah. "John's here, Annie," she told her. "I'm going up to the kitchen to make tea." She patted John's shoulder and smiled reassuringly at him as she started to climb the stairs. "I'll bring some down to you in just a minute."

John sat down on the floor by the cot and took out his flute. "Grandfather has taught me, Annie, that sometimes there are no words to relieve our pain. If you let it, the music may bring you some small comfort." He paused and looked at his friend questioningly. "Would you like for me to play?"

Annie sniffled, wiped her nose with her sleeve, and nodded. "Thank you, John," she said weakly. She closed her eyes, letting the gentle tune float all around her, and finally settling deep within her heart.

In a little while, Miss Susannah returned with steaming cups of tea and warm cinnamon bread. "This is delicious, Miss Susannah," she declared. "I really do feel much better, John. Thank you for staying with me." She took another sip of her tea. "Mama would say that I've got to have faith that the Lord is looking out for me and for them, too. She'd expect me to be strong, and that's what I'm going to do."

"Annie, there's a Cherokee word that I'd like to teach you. It is *hihinalii,* and it means 'You are my friend.' I will do whatever I can to help you." John put his hand on Annie's shoulder, and smiled at her.

Annie struggled to repeat the strange Indian word. "Hihinalii," she whispered softly. "Thank you, John. You are my friend, too."

Although Annie's eyes were rimmed in red from the many tears she'd cried, Miss Susannah noticed that a small spark had returned. Smiling, she said, "Well, I'll take these things back upstairs, and leave you two to another game of sticks. Annie's been practicing, John, so you had better look out!" Gathering up the dishes, Miss Susannah piled them on a tray and made her way back up the cellar stairs.

Once the woman was out of earshot, John decided to tell Annie about the idea he'd had that afternoon. "Annie, I found a small keg of gunpowder out in the Thompsons' barn. If we use it right, I think that it might make the 'jars' and 'trumpets' that we're looking for!"

"How?" Annie asked.

"Today I saw a patch of cane out by the barn. I was thinking that I could use some of it to make you a flute," he said grinning, "but once I found that gunpowder, I thought of an even better use for it. I'll bring some here tomorrow, and we'll get to work." Getting up from the floor, John stretched his legs and smiled down at his friend.

"Get some rest tonight, for tomorrow we're going to rescue your brother. We'll make a diversion that Gideon would be proud of!"

17

Gideon Sticks

John rose early from his pallet beside Gray Hawk's bed. After eating a light breakfast in the sunny kitchen, he returned to his grandfather's bedside to find the old man still sleeping. On the table, John laid the breakfast tray that he'd brought, hoping to entice his grandfather to eat a little bit.

He looks so old, John realized as he watched Gray Hawk sleep. Deep lines marred his grandfather's forehead, and loose flesh sagged in folds around his neck. Smudges of black darkened the skin beneath his eyes. He slept on his back, his mouth thrown wide open to inhale every possible breath, and even then John could hear the old man's lungs rattling as they struggled for air. To the boy it seemed that his grandfather had aged years in just a single night. *What will I do if he dies? I'll be all alone, just like Annie. Could I be as courageous as she is?*

Miss Susannah slipped quietly into the room, interrupting John's thoughts. "I'll sit with him for awhile, John. Gray Hawk would want you to be in the barn helping your people." Gently, she wiped the old man's feverish brow with a cool cloth. "Go now, and I'll tend to your grandfather."

The morning sky was bright blue, and tiny puffs of white clouds floated on the horizon. Rays of the winter sun struggled to thaw the frozen earth. John noticed happily that the snowdrifts were finally melting, making his walk a bit easier. Again he was greeted with a gruesome chorus of hacking coughs as he neared the barn. This morning, however, he was not repulsed by the noise; he was just deeply concerned for his people.

John walked through the narrow aisles of sick beds just as he had yesterday. And again, The People responded to the music he made, and the warm smiles he gave. Singing Brook seemed better, and sat up to sing with him when he came by. He made certain to speak to each person, young and old alike, just as his grandfather would have. In return, he received gentle nods and many words of thanks. Even in their own distress, the people were very worried about Gray Hawk's health.

"He's doing well," John replied to their questions. "But he is concerned about all of you. He will come to visit you when he feels better." Deep in his heart, he hoped that his words were true.

Finally John made his way to the back of the barn where he found the keg of gunpowder untouched. After prying the lid off the small barrel with his knife, John removed his gathering sack from his shoulder. He looked quickly around the room, making sure that his actions were not being observed. Then, using quick movements, he scooped the black powder into his hands and deposited it into his pouch. When he had taken enough, he returned the lid to its proper place. Almost as an afterthought, John grabbed a handful of fuses from a burlap sack tucked behind the kegs. "These should work!" he whispered, tucking them into the pouch. Turning around, he limped unsteadily toward the barn door and back out into the bright sunlight.

A day earlier he had noticed a thick patch of tall cane growing behind the barn. He headed in that direction, knife in hand, wondering if indeed this plan of his would work.

"What are you doing, boy?" Corporal Tidwell interrupted his thoughts, and caused John to jump back in surprise. Sauntering around from the back of the barn, Tidwell laughed at the boy's shocked expression. "Are you up to something you shouldn't be? What are you doing with that knife anyway?"

"I'm just getting some of this cane," John answered honestly. Then, thinking quickly, he added, "I'm making a flute for a friend." Reaching over to a tall pole, John said a brief prayer and then sliced at the cane just as he'd seen his father do.

Tidwell sneered disdainfully at the boy. "Well, isn't that sweet? I heard you in that barn playing that awful music of yours. I thought it was some old tomcat bawling. Your people better enjoy it while they can."

"What do you mean by that?" John asked fearfully.

"Why, we leave tomorrow. Didn't you know? The captain's ordered all of the healthy Indians to move on toward the Mississippi River." He grinned cruelly at John, aware of the pain his words caused. "Your grandfather will stay here with those Thompson people, and you will come with me. Captain Cannon's orders!" Snickering, Tidwell turned and headed back toward the camp. "See you in the morning, boy!" he hollered over his shoulder as he sauntered away.

First things first, John mumbled as he limped toward the cellar door. *I'll take care of Annie and Isaiah first. There will be time tomorrow to deal with Captain Cannon's orders. No matter what he says, though, I'm not leaving my grandfather.*

John opened the cellar door and carefully climbed down the steps, dragging the long pieces of cane with him. Moving quietly, he knocked lightly on the well-hidden door in the false wall and waited for Annie's soft reply. "John, is that you?" she called from within the secret room.

"It's me, Annie. I've brought almost everything that we'll need." John placed his sack on the table and took out the fuses. He showed Annie the powdery black substance and laid the cane poles across the cot. "I've seen the jugs of vinegar that Miss Susannah keeps down here in the cellar, and I know she uses cork to seal them. Have you seen extra corks down here? Oh, and we'll need some kind of sack, like a burlap bag."

"Wait," Annie replied. "I believe she has a little box of corks on the shelf. Let me look." Bending low to get through the small door, Annie went out into the cellar. John heard boxes and crates sliding on the shelves, followed by Annie's exultant cries. "I've got them, John!" Grabbing the box of corks and a burlap sack, Annie crept back into the little room.

John was sitting on her cot, using his knife to cut the cane into sections about six inches long. He sawed along the joint lines that were naturally marked in the cane so that the bottom of each section was sealed. The rest was hollow and perfect for holding gunpowder.

"This is how we'll do it, Annie," John explained. "We'll fill each piece with gunpowder." Carefully, he poured the black substance from his sack. Next, he placed a fuse into the gunpowder so that a length of it stuck out of the top of the cane. Finally, he put a cork in the top, and smiled triumphantly at Annie.

"All we have to do is light the fuse and toss this where we want it to go. It will make enough noise to scare old Master Cooper and his entire family."

Annie smiled back at John, but was still hesitant. "Are you sure this will work, John? Have you ever tried this before?"

"Well, no, not exactly, but it should work perfectly. Mr. Charles taught us all about gunpowder and explosives in class." He grinned confidently at Annie. "Don't worry. I was a very good student!"

The two friends set to work making 'Gideon Sticks,' as John liked to call them. By the time they were finished, they had a dozen of them safely packed in the burlap sack, ready for tonight's attack.

John gathered the remaining cane and put it under his arm. Smiling, he said, "Perhaps I'll make a flute for you with these leftovers. If this plan of ours works, we'll know that these plants were definitely chosen for us by the Great Spirit." Smiling, he limped up the secret staircase. "I'll come back down tonight after Grandfather is asleep. We'll leave then. It should be a clear night but we'll take that little lantern to give us some light. We can use it to start the fuses when we're ready, too.

"Mr. Charles pointed out a path to the Cooper plantation when he was telling me about Isaiah. It leads right over the hill to the west, and should make our journey much shorter." John grinned. "He didn't know he was helping a Cherokee 'Gideon' plan his attack!"

Annie became very serious. "They must not know about this, John. Cooper may come here looking for Isaiah, and they will be safer if they don't know anything." Annie spoke solemnly. "We'll bring Isaiah back here tonight, but in the morning we'll find a new place for him to hide."

John nodded in agreement. "It's our secret, Annie. Now, try to get some rest. I'll be back after everyone's gone to sleep."

It was well after midnight when John returned to the secret room. He found a bright-eyed Annie sitting on her cot, the burlap sack at her feet. She was wrapped in an old coat that Miss Susannah had given her when she first came to the Thompsons. It was much too large, but it would keep her comfortably warm on this cold night. The boots she wore, also a gift from Miss Susannah, were old and scuffed, but the soles were still good and the leather would keep her feet warm and dry.

John hoisted the burlap sack over his shoulder and Annie picked up the little lantern. "We must go quickly," John said unnecessarily. Annie was already making her way through the small door, the large coat feeling big and bulky on her slight frame.

Silently the pair climbed the cellar stairs that led to the outside of the house. The night was cold and clear, as John had predicted, with only a slight breeze moving the pine branches in the nearby woods. Annie's boots left little footprints in the bits of snow still left here and there on the ground. John's moccasin prints could be more easily identified: one soft footprint side by side with a long, flat slide caused by his dragging leg. Fearfully, John realized that his limp might be the one clue that gives their plan away. Cutting a small pine sapling near the trail, John brushed the branch on the path behind him to cover up his footprints.

Looking back, Annie smiled. "That's a good idea, John. I bet even Gideon wouldn't have thought of that!" Finding a branch of her own, Annie brushed away her own tracks. The two continued their journey into the dark night, a sack full of Gideon sticks over one shoulder, and a little lantern to light their way.

18
Fighting the Midianites

The Cooper plantation stood black and silent in the dark, the main house guarding its grounds like a sentinel. The winter night, an ebony blanket spread across the sky, camouflaged the building's shabbiness; peeling paint and rotting wood were not visible in the darkness. No light shone from the large windows that stared down at John and Annie like great, lifeless eyes. For the first time since they'd begun their adventure, the young people felt fingers of fear creeping into their hearts.

Moving stealthily to the side of the house, Annie spied the dependencies, the small buildings that served as kitchen, laundry, and blacksmith shop for the plantation. Staring deeper into the darkness, she thought she could just make out the slave quarters; tiny cabins crouched low in a pine thicket behind the stables.

"Annie," John's whisper startled her. She nearly dropped the lantern. "Be careful!" he warned her, as the light teetered in the darkness.

"I'm sorry," she hissed. "You scared me, that's all!" Bending low, she followed John to some thick bushes beside the house. There they sat, placing the lantern between them. Huddled together in the prickly branches of the holly plants, John explained his plan to Annie.

"This is what we'll do," John spoke softly, but authoritatively. "We'll light the fuses, throw the 'sticks' toward the front of the house, and wait for everyone to run in the direction of the noise.

"When I tell you to, run toward the slave quarters as fast as you can. Stay low to the ground, but keep an eye out for Isaiah. I'll meet you back at the trail."

Annie nodded, but the fingers of fear she had felt moments ago were nothing compared to the fist of terror that now gripped her chest. "I'm ready," she whispered bravely, and John lit the first fuse.

He tossed it far into the woods on the opposite side of the broad front lawn and waited for the explosion. It came seconds later, along with a bright flash of light and a cloud of smoke. In the darkness, Annie could just make out John's mischievous grin. "I knew they would work!" Quickly the pair lit one fuse after another, and soon the woods teemed with wild bursts of noise and the fearful shouts of terrified people.

"What the devil's going on out here?" Stuart Cooper yelled from between the tall columns of his grand front porch. He was barefooted, and dressed in only a rumpled night shirt. His riotous mane of gray hair put Annie in mind of a terrified porcupine, and she had to stifle a laugh.

"Now, Annie, go!" John shoved her gently, pushing her out of their hiding place. He continued firing off the little bombs, one after another, keeping the mayhem on the Cooper plantation at a fevered pitch.

Annie ran toward the slave cabins, hiding in the shadows as much as possible. She kept her eyes on the faces of the panicked slaves, however, always looking for the familiar form of her brother.

"Isaiah," she called softly over and over again. No one heard her, so intent were they on getting to the source of the strange noises. Some even pushed past her, brushing her arm as they ran, but still no one seemed to notice her.

Finally, she felt a hand grab hers, and joyfully she recognized Isaiah's calloused fingers as they pulled her toward the back of one of the cabins.

"Isaiah!" she cried out softly, throwing her arms around his neck. "I found you! You must come with me. John will be waiting at the path." Grabbing his hand, she tugged him toward the woods.

"Wait, Annie! How did you find me? Who's John?" Realizing that now was not the time for questions, Isaiah stopped talking and simply followed his sister, running for his life towards the darkened path.

The little explosions had ceased now, and the woods on the far side of the plantation were alight with lanterns and torches. Apparently, Mr. Cooper had ordered everyone out of their beds and into the trees to find the source of this midnight irritation. John grabbed the burlap bag, and made his way back to the trail, grinning with satisfaction. He found Annie and Isaiah, breathless but smiling, waiting for him.

"You need to hurry," John told them. "Cooper will be counting his slaves, looking for runaways. We need to get Isaiah to safety as quickly as possible. Don't wait for me, Annie. I can't keep up with you and your brother. Run now, and I'll meet up with you later."

Isaiah began to protest, but Annie quickly silenced him. "He's right, Isaiah," she told him. "All of our work tonight will be for nothing if they catch you. Let's go!" John watched, smiling as the brother and sister ran through the darkness to the safety of the tiny secret room.

Over in the east, John could see the telltale streaks of dawn, slashes of light in the brightening sky. A dark shadow sailed silently above him, circling once before winging its way toward the west. *An owl,* John realized, *returning home from an evening of hunting. I hope he was as successful as we were!*

From his vantage point at the top of the hill, the boy looked down on the Thompson house, surprised to see lights on in each room. He recognized the black carriage of the doctor from Hopkinsville tied in up in front, and realized suddenly that something was terribly wrong.

The owl! It was a sign! John thought with dismay. *There's been a death! Grandfather!* With tears streaming down his face, the boy hurried down the hill. But in his heart he already knew that he was too late. His grandfather was gone.

Miss Susannah rushed to the door when she heard John on the front porch. She clutched him to her, pressing his head against her shoulder. He felt her warm, wet tears on his face as they ran down her cheeks. No words were necessary.

The doctor walked slowly into the room where John and Miss Susannah stood in a silent, tearful embrace. "I'm so sorry, John," the old doctor said kindly. "We did everything that we could for your grandfather. Miss Susannah was with him when he slipped into unconsciousness. Mr. Charles came for me right away, but there was nothing else anyone could do." Knowing that his words could not bring comfort to the grieving boy, the doctor patted John's shoulder, then turned and left through the front door.

"Please, Miss Susannah, may I go to him?" John asked, his tear-streaked face turned up to hers.

"Of course, John. Come with me," she replied, and walked with him down the hall. John entered the room silently with his head bowed, and waited while Susannah closed the door behind him. She understood that John needed this private time with Gray Hawk, to be alone with him, to say good-bye.

When John emerged from the room an hour later, he found Charles and Susannah waiting for him in the kitchen. His eyes were red from crying, and his face was now streaked with soot from the wood stove. Susannah looked at him questioningly, but John explained that it was the custom of The People. "I will wear this soot for many days," he explained, "to honor the memory of my grandfather. This morning I will go into the woods to get willow root so that I can prepare his body for burial."

"I'll go with you, John," Charles said, rising from the table where he and Susannah had been drinking tea. "It would be an honor to help you with this, if you would let me." John nodded, and the boy and the man donned their heavy jackets to brave the cold winter morning.

Susannah made her way down the steps to the secret room. She had been so busy caring for Gray Hawk that she had not had time to speak with Annie. She was shocked to see Isaiah sitting on his cot, playing "sticks" with his sister.

"Isaiah!" she shrieked with delight. "However did you get here?"

"Sit down, Miss Susannah, and let me tell you the courageous story of this wonderful sister of mine and her very inventive friend!" he said. And Isaiah told the entire story, pride in his sister's bravery glowing in his eyes. Annie's face beamed with happiness at her brother's words.

When Isaiah finished, Miss Susannah told the two siblings about Gray Hawk. Tears made watery tracks down Annie's face as she listened to the sad news. "But John was with me, helping to rescue Isaiah," she lamented. "He should have been here instead, taking care of Gray Hawk. This is all my fault." Covering her face with her hands, Annie wept softly.

Sitting on the little bed next to her, Miss Susannah spoke gently. "No, Annie," she said. "John doesn't blame you. He blames himself, actually. But it's not anyone's fault. There was nothing we could do." Wiping a tear from her own cheek, Miss Susannah said quietly, "It was just Gray Hawk's time. His heart could not bear staying in this world any longer. He's at peace now, and we must help John understand that."

When Charles and John returned from the woods, Susannah helped the boy prepare the boiling willow root for the ceremonial cleansing of Gray Hawk's body. John performed the cleansing by himself; this duty was his alone. As he carried the boiling liquid into the room to perform the necessary task, he turned and looked at the Thompsons.

"I thank you for being here with him when he died. You are such good friends. I will need your help later this afternoon as I prepare a tomb for him." Charles and Susannah silently nodded in unison, and John once again entered his grandfather's room, closing the door quietly behind him.

He sat for a long time at his grandfather's side, studying the peaceful expression on the old man's face. Gray Hawk seemed so content now, so restful. Through his own grief, John forced himself to remember that his grandfather was now in a much better place full of light and loved ones.

Perhaps he is with my grandmother now, and my parents. He thought through a cloud of sadness. *Can you see me now, Grandfather? Will your spirit stay here with me for just a little while?* Closing his eyes, and taking his grandfather's still hand, John repeated the prayer he'd heard Gray Hawk pray for The People so many times.

Great Spirit, whose voice I hear in the wind, whose breath gives life to all the world; Hear me, I need your strength and wisdom to see me through these difficult days.

Laying his head on his grandfather's shoulder and gently draping his arms around Gray Hawk's body, John wept until he had no tears left to shed.

19
Canku Ota

Captain Cannon knocked gently on the door of the Thompsons' home. It was still early morning, but news of Gray Hawk's death had already spread throughout the Cherokee camp. Miss Susannah opened the door and invited the captain inside.

"I've come to see John." Captain Cannon spoke softly and removed his hat politely as he entered the sitting room. The grief in the house was palpable; it poured over him like cold water, chilling him to the very bone. "I'm so sorry about Gray Hawk. He was a good man, a leader for his people, and he will be sorely missed."

Smiling sadly, Miss Susannah offered the captain a chair, and went down the hall to get John. Peering into the dimly lit room where John still sat with Gray Hawk's body, Miss Susannah whispered to the boy, "Captain Cannon is here to see you, John. Will you come out and speak to him?"

Nodding, John followed her down the hall and into the light of the sitting room. He blinked, trying to adjust to the brightness. His red-rimmed eyes were swollen, and they stung from all the tears that they had shed. Streaks of black soot remained on his face, but had been smeared by crying. Still, he stood tall and proud, extending his hand in a gesture of welcome to the uniformed officer. Standing to shake John's hand, Captain Cannon's heart broke for this brave, forlorn young man.

"Please accept the condolences of the United States government,

John. We, the soldiers and the officers, are all very saddened by his death." He hesitated just a moment before continuing. "As you know, we were planning to continue on our march to the Oklahoma Territory today. However, under the circumstances, we will delay one more day so that all of The People can pay their respects to your grandfather." He looked solemnly at John, waiting for his response.

"Thank you, Captain," he replied. "I will prepare a burial place for my grandfather this afternoon. Please tell The People that we will meet at sundown for a ceremony."

"I will, John," the captain assured him. As Captain Cannon turned to leave, he patted the boy's shoulder and spoke to him gently. "Gray Hawk would be impressed with the courage you are displaying during this difficult time. He was very proud to be your grandfather." He nodded to Miss Susannah, and strode through the front door into the cold, clear day.

Later that morning, Charles accompanied John outside in search of a proper resting place for Gray Hawk. They finally decided to use the large rock, Charles' hiding place for his disguise and walking stick. Together they built three stone walls, each about eighteen inches high, using the large rock for the fourth wall. According to tradition, Gray Hawk's body should be positioned to face the west, the usunhiyi or 'darkening land.' John laid sacred cedar branches on the ground where the body would rest. When the tomb was ready, John and Charles returned to the house to wait.

An elder from each of the Cherokee clans arrived at the Thompson's door late that afternoon, followed by a group of the principal women. The men gently lifted Gray Hawk's body from the bed and carried it through the front door and down the steps. The women began their ceremonial weeping as the body passed them and continued the mournful crying as they followed the men to the tomb near the edge of the woods.

Many of The People had gathered to honor Gray Hawk. To John's surprise, a large group of soldiers was also in attendance, headed by

Captain Cannon, who stood respectfully at a distance. The Cherokee wept openly for their beloved leader, while the soldiers stood with heads bowed, hats in their hands as a sign of respect.

Prayers were offered by the elders, and songs were sung. Musicians played mournful melodies that pierced the hearts of all in attendance. Finally, just as the sun was setting, John placed his flute to his lips and played a haunting refrain that would forever serve as his final farewell to his grandfather. As he played, tears welled in the eyes of many, but not a sound was heard except for the piercing notes of John's mournful dirge. When he had finished, each Cherokee took a small cedar branch, and laid it gently on top of Gray Hawk's body. Then the elders added large wooden planks to the top of the tomb. Finally rocks were placed on the very top, sealing the burial place forever. The People dispersed in silence, returning to their tents and shelters to prepare for the journey the following day.

Singing Brook, who had recovered from her illness in time to travel on with her family, approached John shyly. "These are for you, John. My mother said that these beads will comfort your heart." She handed John a small package wrapped in a frayed cloth. Inside, John found a strand of beads of various colors and sizes, strung together on a narrow leather cord.

"Thank you, Singing Brook," John said, the words catching in his throat as he spoke. "The beads are very beautiful, and I will keep them close to my heart always." Tying the leather strip around his neck, John smiled down at the little girl. She smiled back, threw her arms around his waist, and hugged him fiercely. Then turning away, she ran the short distance to where her mother stood, watching.

Charles walked over to John, and placed his arm around the boy's shoulder. "Gray Hawk taught me so much about your people and your customs, John. He taught me about strength and wisdom, too." His arm remained around the boy as he guided him back toward the house. "Gray Hawk told me once about 'canku ota' or 'many paths.' He told me that each of us has many journeys to make in this life, many trails to follow. I'm so glad that your path led you here to us." The white man and the Indian boy walked together in the dying winter light, comforted by their love for each other.

Annie and Isaiah had crept upstairs to watch the ceremony from the little window in the kitchen. When they saw that the mourners were leaving, they darted back down the secret stairs to the safety of the hidden room.

"How terrible for John, to lose his grandfather while traveling on this awful journey," Isaiah said, compassion for his new friend evident in the tremors of his voice. "What would we do if that happened to us, Annie?"

Annie looked down at the dirt floor, unable to meet her brother's eyes. She had not told Isaiah about her parents and Jacob, so frightened was she that he'd leave her to go find them. She was right to be afraid.

"Isaiah, I need to tell you something," Annie began slowly. Sitting beside him on his cot, she told him the entire story without stopping and without looking up. At the end, she said pleadingly, "Please don't leave me again, Isaiah. If you want to go after them, I'll go with you. I could be a help to you on the road, and you wouldn't have to be alone." But when she looked up into his face, she knew his decision had already been made.

Gently, Isaiah took her small hands in his. "Annie," he said, "I have to go find them, and you know that I have to go alone. It's too dangerous for you." Looking deeply into her eyes, he continued, "Mama and Papa would want you to get to the North, just like we planned. They would want you to get an education, to build a life for yourself. The Thompsons will help you get to freedom, and you'll be safe."

Annie knew that any objection she voiced would fall on deaf ears. She sat stock still, realizing that her life was about to take a very different path indeed. She was about to embark on a journey of her own, all by herself, to a place she'd never seen. A sad smile teased the corners of her mouth. *Just like John,* she mused. She was terrified at the thought.

Later that evening, the Thompsons came down to talk to Isaiah and Annie. "You'll be leaving us tomorrow," Charles told them. "I've made arrangements for you to travel by wagon to Madisonville, and then on from there to Cape Girardeau." He paused momentarily, and studied the young people carefully. "This may be a difficult trip, Isaiah. There is always danger of capture by slave catchers, so you must constantly be on the alert. Annie is strong and resourceful, but this is not a journey for anyone to have to make on their own."

Alarmed, Annie opened her mouth to protest. "But Mr. Charles, Isaiah is not going with me. He's leaving tomorrow to find our parents. I'm going to have to make this trip alone!"

Charles turned to Isaiah, "Is this true, young man? Do you realize the danger that you'll be facing if you return to the South?"

"I understand," the boy answered slowly, considering. "It's a chance I'm willing to take. Somebody has got to help my family, and I'm the only one who can do it." He got up from his cot, and paced, his long legs making short work of the little room. "Is there another way to get Annie to the North? A way that would be safer for her?"

Suddenly all heads turned toward the top of the stairs where the telltale sound of the secret door opening had caught their attention. The Thompsons looked at each other in alarm. Annie's heart was pounding out of her chest, and even Isaiah's eyes were wide with fear. "Mr. Charles? Miss Susannah? Are you there?" John called down from above.

"John, you scared the devil out of us!" Charles exclaimed. Four relieved sighs were heard as the Cherokee boy hobbled down the steps. "We thought you were resting!"

"I was," John replied sheepishly, "but I woke up and it was

very quiet, and a little lonely." His eyes were no longer red, and he looked rested and strong. He limped to the small stool and sat down. "I guess I just didn't want to be alone right now."

Charles smiled gently. "You're always welcome here with us, John. Maybe you can help us solve a problem with Isaiah and Annie."

Miss Susannah had been quiet for quite some time, pondering the situation. Suddenly, she cried out excitedly, "Charles, wait! I know what to do! This is a plan that's sure to work!" Quickly, she explained her idea to the little group.

Grinning, Charles rose from his perch on the cot beside Isaiah, and headed up the staircase. In a few moments he was out the door, on his way to see Captain Cannon.

Later that night after his meeting with Charles Thompson, Captain Cannon entered the following words in his journal:

February 15, 1839: Attended burial service for Gray Hawk, great leader of the Cherokee people. His death was due to complications associated with pneumonia. Age at time of death uncertain. Party will continue march to Oklahoma Territory tomorrow after three week delay while many Cherokee recovered from illnesses. Charles Thompson requested that John, grandson of Gray Hawk, be allowed to remain in their home so that he can minister to the Indians still unable to travel. I gave permission, with the understanding that John will join his people in Oklahoma at a later date. Thompson agreed to my terms.

Smiling, Captain Cannon put his pen down and closed his journal. *That will be the official report,* he thought slyly. *I'm grateful to Charles for being honest with me. It's a good work that the Thompsons are doing here. I know John will be a help to them, wherever he is.*

* * *

Isaiah stood in the morning mist, hugging his sister. Tears were threatening to spill from the eyes of both brother and sister as they stepped back from their embrace. "I'll find you, Annie," Isaiah assured her. "Be careful, and do what the Thompsons tell you to do." Annie nodded silently.

"Isaiah, take this," Mr. Charles said, handing him a small paper. On it was written in careful manuscript the letters S-I-N-O-N. "When you get to Cape Girardeau, find a steamship painted white with black trim. It will have these letters written on the side. The captain of that ship is a friend of mine, and he will help you find Annie." He embraced the boy gently and then handed him a small packet of money. "May God go with you," he said softly.

Isaiah walked slowly down the path. At the crossroad, he headed south, turning to wave once again to his sister. "I love you, Isaiah," Annie called to him as he disappeared in the grayness of the dawn. She was glad for the darkness; it hid the tears she did not wish for her brother to see.

20

The Flying Fishers Traveling Circus

"Come, Annie," Miss Susannah said softly, as she steered the girl back toward the house. "It's time we get you and John ready for your trip. The wagon will be here soon."

An hour later, after gorging themselves on the huge breakfast that Miss Susannah had prepared, John and Annie found themselves being loaded onto a large wagon filled with hay. Annie was wearing the oversized coat once more, thankful for its warmth. Miss Susannah had crammed food into the enormous pockets of the coat and had given John extra packets of bread and dried meat to store in his gathering sack. Wrapped in quilts, the children were hidden deep within the piles of hay, eager for this trip to begin.

"We humbly ask protection for these young people," Annie heard Mr. Charles pray. "Be with them and guide them on this dangerous journey. Carry them safely in the palm of your hand, O Lord. Amen."

"Amen," echoed the wagon driver, a young man wearing a black coat, heavy gloves, and a battered brown hat. Without another word, the wagon jerked forward roughly, and Annie and John were on their way. They stopped momentarily at what Annie figured to be the crossroad at the bottom of the path. Suddenly she felt the horses pull again, heading north, away from her brother and her family, and away from the Thompsons, the special friends she had grown to love.

John lay quietly in the sweet-smelling hay. He was thinking about the conversation he'd had last night with Mr. Charles. The man had been insistent that John travel along with Annie to the North. But John had protested. "What about my people?" he asked earnestly. "Wouldn't Grandfather want me to go with them? Who will help care for them if they get sick?"

Mr. Charles considered carefully before he answered. "John, I think that your grandfather would be proud of you for helping this young girl find her freedom.

"Gray Hawk watched in horror as his own people became enslaved to the United States government, unable to fight for their freedom. Wouldn't he be pleased that his grandson not only understood the injustice of slavery but was willing to take a stand against it?"

John did not know the answer to that. He lay on his bed that night pondering Mr. Charles' words. Finally, exhausted by the events of the day and the struggles he had yet to face, John fell into a deep sleep. Far into the night he dreamed that Gray Hawk spoke to him.

In the dream, John was walking down a long, narrow path. The branches of large oak trees formed a canopy over his head, blocking the sunlight. Suddenly, Grandfather appeared to him as a figure in white, an undulating phantom floating just out of John's reach. "My grandson," the quavering voice spoke slowly, "do not be afraid to help the Thompsons. Do not turn away from this girl in her time of need."

"But, Grandfather," John replied, his dream now seeming eerily real, "what will happen to The People?"

"Do not fear for them, John. The Great Spirit watches over them and you." As the specter floated slowly away toward the western sky, John heard it utter one more word. "Tadeyastatakuhl!" it whispered, and was gone.

Amazingly, John slept soundly the rest of the night. When he awoke in the morning, he understood that traveling with Annie was the right decision. He knew, deep within his heart, that Grand-father had given his approval.

So now, in the breaking dawn of this cold February day, John and Annie were warm and safe, wrapped in blankets beneath the hay. Talking was difficult, so they lay companionably side by side, allowing the steady plodding of the horses and the soft singing of their young driver to gently lull them to sleep.

* * *

Sometime in mid-afternoon, the wagon's sudden stop jarred Annie awake. The driver had stopped his singing. She lay motionless, listening. Presently the voices of men arguing filled her ears, and she became frightened. Through the piles of hay, she could just make out John's face, and she saw her fear mirrored in his eyes. Putting a finger to his lips, John motioned for her to remain silent. Reaching through the hay, he grabbed her hand and squeezed. Annie held on tightly, then closed her eyes and waited.

Two men were yelling at the driver, their words coarse and cruel. It seems that they wanted some of his hay for their horses, but were not eager to pay for it. "You might as well give it to us, boy," the first man sneered. Annie could hear his disdain even through the hay and blanket.

"Come on," said the second man. "You've got plenty to spare, and we know you won't fight us for it." He laughed mockingly at the driver, who had not yet uttered a word.

Chills ran up and down Annie's spine. *I know that voice!* She realized suddenly. *That's Willie Hall!* By carefully moving bits of straw, Annie made a small tunnel through which she could view the two men. *It is him!* She wanted to scream.

The men began to help themselves to the hay. Quickly, John pulled Annie down deeper into the wagon, drawing her under the blankets. The men scooped their stolen hay into burlap sacks, their hands barely grazing the blankets hiding the two passengers. John and Annie both held their breath, praying that they would not be discovered.

"Wouldn't do that if I were you," the driver said with a sternness and confidence that stopped the bandits in their tracks. "You see, gentlemen, we are passing through the jurisdiction of Crittenden County. My uncle Michael Shay is the sheriff here, and I'm sure he would not be pleased to have a horse thief and his partner on the loose in his territory." The young man lied convincingly. Quickly grabbing hold of Willie's arm, the driver turned it so that the HT was clearly visible on the criminal's thumb.

Through the hay, Annie saw the glimmer of the shiny barrel of a shotgun, and realized that their young driver had been prepared for an incident like this. One good look at his gun and the threat of a sheriff's posse had apparently been enough to scare off Willie Hall and his cowardly partner. They bolted off, a couple of frightened rabbits, lost in a cloud of dust. John grinned at Annie, and they both relaxed, feeling safe in the courageous protection of their young driver, who was once again humming his happy tune.

Hours later, outside of Madisonville the wagon finally stopped for the night. "C'mon!" the young man called to the pair. "It's safe to get out now!" Crawling out from under the hay, Annie and John were amazed at the sight before them.

They were in the middle of a huge field. Before them stood an enormous canvas tent, its large flaps opened wide to reveal brightly painted wooden benches scattered around the edges of a swept dirt floor. Men and women of all shapes, colors, and sizes stood about talking and laughing. Musicians were busily packing up their instruments, while an assortment of unusual animals was being led through the back of the tent by their trainers.

"What is that?" Annie shrieked. She wasn't sure if she felt terror or delight as she pointed at the huge gray animal with its flapping ears and enormous legs. It stood at least ten feet tall. At that very moment it was lumbering toward the wagon; the huge appendage protruding from the middle of its face seemed to be waving a greeting at their driver. Both children stared in amazement, mouths open wide.

"Why, this is Sarah Josepha, the smartest elephant to ever walk the face of the earth! Isn't she a beauty? She's come all the way from India!" the young man boasted, jumping down from his perch on the wagon seat. Grabbing a handful of the fresh hay, he ran over to the mammoth animal, and handed her the treat. He motioned to John and Annie. "C'mon! Haven't you seen an elephant before?" John and Annie looked at each other and shook their heads. Dumbfounded, they returned their gaze to the monster before them.

"She won't bite! She's as gentle as a little lamb! And she's so smart that I'm teaching her to walk the tightrope!" he laughed as his two passengers moved hesitantly toward the animal, their eyes intently watching every move the elephant made. Neither Annie nor John relished the idea of being crushed under the feet of such a massive beast.

"We named her after the famous lady who wrote that poem about Mary and her little lamb. You know the one:

> 'Mary had a little lamb,
> its fleece was white as snow,
> and everywhere that Mary went,
> the lamb was sure to go!'

"Sarah Josepha is sort of a long name though, so we usually just call her Josie," the boy explained, patting the beast's head affectionately. "We would have named her Mary, but that's the fat lady's name," he winked mischievously, "and we thought it might get confusing."

"I heard that, young man!" called out a roly-poly red-haired lady. She looked like a little pink mountain as she waddled awkwardly up to the children. Her huge dress was a rosy cascade of bows and ruffles. She wore matching ribbons in her auburn curls and tiny pink slippers on her feet. Her cherry-red cheeks were puffed out in a childish pout, but she couldn't disguise the amused gleam in her bright brown eyes.

"What mischief are you up to now?" she asked, fondly poking the boy in his ribs. "And who are your new friends?" Mary extended her hand first to Annie and then to John. As the two introduced themselves, Mary shook each hand vigorously. "Nice to meet you," her voice sang out. "Now, watch out for our little trouble-maker here," she smiled, gesturing at the boy by her side, "Make sure that he doesn't drag you into any of his foolhardy plans!" With that, Mary trundled off toward her wagon.

"Love you, Mary!" the boy called after her. And by the affection that could be seen gleaming brightly in his eyes, it was obvious that he did.

"Come on now, Annie," he spoke encouragingly. "Give Josie a chance."

Bravely, Annie slowly approached the animal. She gently touched the beast's face, and was astounded when the elephant carefully wrapped its long trunk around her shoulders. Annie smiled delightedly.

"See! Gentle as can be! That a girl, Sarah Josepha!" the young man exclaimed, grinning broadly. "Since Josie seems to like you so much, I guess I better introduce myself. My name is Douglas Alexander Nettles, but everybody around here calls me Dan."

With a wide sweep of his hand, and deep bow, Dan spoke dramatically as if addressing an audience. "Welcome, Annie and John, to the greatest little show east of the Mississippi River: The Flying Fishers Traveling Circus and Exotic Menagerie!"

* * *

Clayton Collins and Abraham Lincoln sat together talking in the cluttered law office.

"Don't you still have relatives down in Kentucky, Abraham?" Clayton asked his troubled friend. "This would be a perfect opportunity to visit with them, and you would be doing a great favor for an old friend." Clayton smiled fondly at the young lawyer. "It would also put a little extra gold in that empty pocket of yours."

Abraham couldn't deny the truth in that statement. Clayton was right; his money was almost gone and he could use the extra work. Clayton's firm was representing a very fussy old woman who had some legal work that needed to be done in Wickliffe, Kentucky. It would be just a short boat ride down the Mississippi from Cape Girardeau. And one thing about the persnickety woman: she paid her lawyers extremely well.

"Fine," Abraham agreed. "At least it will delay a very difficult conversation with my landlady. I'm not looking forward to telling that sweet lady that her precious son is nothing more than a common horse thief."

Clayton smiled, his green eyes twinkling. "I figured I could convince you. I've already booked passage for you on a steamship headed to Wickliffe. It's nothing fancy, but it'll get you there!"

And so, the very next morning, a surprised Abraham found himself once again aboard *The Sinon* with his friend, Captain Richardson.

21

A Face Like Grimaldi

"Would you two like to see the rest of the animals?" Dan asked John and Annie as he led them around to the back of the enormous tent. "We keep them there, in their wagons." He pointed to half a dozen large painted carts with caged windows. Each wagon was decorated with colorful paintings of the occupants, complete with huge claws, bloody fangs, and wild eyes.

If the pictures are half as frightening as the animals, I don't think I want to look inside those cages! Annie thought, taking a step back from the two boys.

John, on the other hand, was intrigued. "What kinds of animals are these?" he asked.

"Well, we have your basic circus fare," Dan boasted, "with a few exotic ones to really stir up the audience." He walked toward a golden-yellow wagon decorated with what appeared to be an enormous cat. In the painting, the cat's jaws were opened in an angry roar, as if ready to gobble up the first human who came near. Annie shuddered, but John just grinned.

"Can we touch him?" he asked Dan.

"Touch him!" Dan replied. "Don't even get near him! This is our lion, the King of the Jungle, a real man-eater, and I'm not sure he's been fed today!" As Dan got closer to the wagon, the lion let out his fierce roar, and John jumped back in fear.

"I think I'll stay back here," he muttered.

Dan smiled. "Let me show you the rest," he said. "They're not quite as ferocious!"

He led John and Annie from wagon to wagon, describing each animal's diet and care. The two youngsters were treated to their first looks at a panther, a kangaroo, and a boa constrictor, touted as "the strangling serpent." They watched as the animal trainers managed a small group of zebras, gathering them into a circle and commanding them to run around and around until their black and white striped bodies all blurred together in Annie's eyes. But their favorite, besides Josie, was the little rhinoceros named Bert. The Flying Fishers advertised him as "the amazing unicorn" because of the strange horn he bore on the front of his head.

"Dan!" a very loud male voice thundered across the field. Through the semidarkness, Annie could just make out the frame of a tall, lanky man walking toward them. "We need your help with the ropes, boy. This work won't get done by itself!" He threw his arm affectionately around Dan's neck, and ruffled his hair with his hand. "But first, introduce me to our new friends."

"Annie and John, this is Jackson Fisher," Dan spoke politely and respectfully. "He's the owner of this circus and the star of the Flying Fishers, the famous trapeze artists." With a wink and a grin, Dan added, "You can just call him Jack."

"We're glad to have you both with us," Jack said, his deep brown eyes filled with compassion as he spoke. He placed his hand on John's shoulder, and smiled at Annie. "My parents, the original Flying Fishers, began helping Africans escape from slavery many years ago. They were proud to use their circus as part of this Underground Railroad. My brother, sisters, and I practically grew up with runaways at our door."

"And now you're continuing the tradition," John said, smiling.

"We are grateful for your help, Jack." Annie added.

"Did you have any trouble with our 'cargo'?" the man asked, nodding toward John and Annie.

Shaking his head, Dan replied, "Just a couple of bandits after some of Josie's hay. Nothing I couldn't handle."

A knowing look passed between Annie and John.

"What?" Jack asked. "Is there something you're not telling us?"

Annie's eyes filled with tears, and she turned her face toward the ground. John put his arm around her shoulders, and told their friends about Willie and Isaiah. He ended by telling them about Annie's parents and her little brother.

"Annie," Jack said soothingly, "I hope that your family is re-united very soon. Know that while you're here with us, we're your family, too."

He hugged Annie, and smiled at John over the top of her head. "That goes for you, too, young man!" he said, and winked at the Cherokee lad.

The sun had now set behind the Kentucky hills, and pinpricks of starlight were beginning to poke through the velvety sky. Many of the circus folk were bustling around, packing away possessions, tending to animals, and preparing for the evening's journey.

"We'd like to stand around here and talk some more," Jack said, eyeing the darkening sky, "but Dan has lots of work to do before we'll be ready to move out. We're supposed to be ready for the Wickliffe parade by mid-morning tomorrow. Let's get moving, boy!"

Dan took off running toward the inside of the canvas tent where a crew was already working to disassemble the cloth structure. Torches held aloft in large sconces illuminated the circus yard as men, women, and animals made ready for the move.

"Why are we traveling so late?" Annie asked Jack, as she and John followed him across the field. "Wouldn't it be easier to leave in the morning when everyone is rested?"

"Annie, that would seem logical except," Jack paused, then added, "we want the people of the towns to actually have to pay their money to see our animals. If we travel during the day, it would be difficult to hide our menagerie. So, we cover up their wagons at night, and slip them as quietly down these country roads as we possibly can. Darkness is the perfect cover!"

Annie grinned. "For us, too! It's much easier to carry two secret 'packages' like us at night than in broad daylight!"

"Exactly," Jack nodded in agreement. "You can see now why the Flying Fishers have made such great conductors for the Underground Railroad."

He stopped in front of a large wagon that looked like a little wooden box on four wheels. It was painted pink with white trim and reminded Annie of the peppermint candy she'd seen through the windows of fancy stores in town. The wagon's door was ajar even in the cool evening air, and bright lights shone through tiny windows. Annie and John heard a familiar voice call from inside.

"Come on in, you two! You'll be riding with me tonight and we're going to have a grand time!" The young people smiled at Mary's enthusiastic welcome and climbed the little steps into the wagon.

"Mary will take good care of you," Jack assured them with a smile. "We'll be loaded up and ready to start out in an hour or so. Could you get them something to eat, Mary?"

"Be happy to!" came Mary's cheery reply. "Something nice and hearty for your bellies now, I think, and then a little rest. In the morning, we'll fix each of you up to look like just another member of our traveling troupe!"

After a simple but delicious supper of warm brown bread and hot soup, John and Annie curled up in blankets on the floor of Mary's little wagon. It was cramped quarters, but cozy, and the constant rocking of the wagon quickly soothed the exhausted youngsters into a deep sleep.

They did not open their eyes until the next morning when the wagon train finally stopped in a large meadow outside the city limits of Wickliffe. Darkness lay like a tattered blanket over the little circus camp; daylight was just beginning to filter through the frayed edges of the gray sky. The wagon's windowpanes were frosty; it was a chilly February morning in Kentucky.

"Annie! John!" Dan hollered as he shook the sleeping pair. "Wake up! We've got to get you ready!" On a three-legged stool beside him sat tiny pots of paint, all different colors. On the floor were garments of various sizes and textures, as if a little old lady's trunk had exploded like one of John's Gideon sticks. Torn silk scarves lay tangled with cheap glass bead necklaces, and the floppy soles of old men's shoes trampled crumpled felt hats. A lacy lavender dress, probably worn generations ago, danced stiffly on a hook beside a pair of patched men's britches that hung, ungallantly, by their worn suspenders.

"What is all this?" a groggy Annie asked Dan. John simply sat, rubbing his eyes, and staring at the mess.

"We're going to make you clowns!" Dan announced. "Just like me! Once I get the makeup and costumes on you two, you'll have the perfect disguises!" And so, Dan set to work.

First he selected costumes. For Annie he chose the lavender dress, long white gloves, and tall white boots that buttoned up the front. Around her neck he draped strand after strand of bright glass beads. Stepping back, he examined her from head to toe. "We must be sure that no skin is showing, Annie. That would ruin everything, and give away our deception," Dan told her, his face serious.

Next he began to work on her makeup. Pulling back her wavy hair, he tied it with a cherry-red scarf. He placed a large floppy straw hat on her head, and tucked her hair underneath. Taking a small pot from the stool, he removed the lid and began spreading white paint all over her face, ears, and neck. Annie grimaced at the sticky feel of the stuff being spread across her skin.

"This is the way a 'whiteface' circus clown makes up his face. A man named Joseph Grimaldi started doing this a few years back in England, and now just about every clown does it," Dan explained as he continued working on Annie's face. "Next, we'll add some color to your eyes here," he touched her eyebrows and eyelids with dark black, forming pointed triangles, "and we'll finish with a huge red mouth. Take a look!" Dan held a large mirror for Annie to view her new face. "Oh, my!" was all that Annie could say as she turned her face left and right to examine the strange sight before her. John and Dan laughed at her bewilderment.

"Now, sit right over there and be still, Miss Annie, or your paint will smear and we'll have to start all over." Annie tried to do as she was told, but the paint felt heavy on her skin, and as it dried it began to itch. It took all of her self-control to keep her gloved hands in her lap, not scratching her itchy face.

Dan was busy selecting a costume for John. He picked the colorfully patched men's pants with their striped suspenders, a thick muslin shirt with long sleeves and high collar, and heavy black boots that had obviously traveled many, many miles. Dan wrapped John's hair in a bright red bandana, and then topped it with a wide-brimmed hat. Only John's face was visible; every other inch of his skin was covered.

Taking the paint pot again, Dan smeared the sticky stuff over John's face and neck. John sat quiet and still, enduring the ordeal, until Dan finished and held the mirror up for his inspection. The transformation was amazing. John's mouth was painted red, but not in the huge smile that Annie wore. Instead, his lips were painted in a frown. One blue tear was painted delicately on John's cheek. "I could not disguise your grief," Dan told John quietly, "even with all the funny paint in the world."

As with Annie, Dan had added a dark black triangle above and below each of John's eyes. "The black triangles are very important," Dan announced solemnly. "They will help your guide recognize you. When he sees your faces painted like this, he'll know that you're his next passengers."

Annie stared at Dan in surprise. "Do you mean to say that he'll be at the parade today in Wickliffe?"

"That's right," Dan replied. "You'll be leaving the parade to go with him. He is the captain of a steamship that is docked on the river. He'll be waiting for you."

"Now," Dan announced, wiping his hands on a damp rag, "I must go get myself ready. The parade will begin in just a little while, and the three of us will be the stars of the show!"

22

Leah, the Learned Pig

Neither Annie nor John would have recognized Dan in his wonderful clown costume. Dan's face, like theirs, was painted snow white with striking red cheeks and upturned lips. On his head he wore a bushy wig of curly orange hair topped with a cone-shaped hat of swirling blues, reds, and yellows. His costume was a one-piece coverall, also snowy white, with gloves and slippers that matched. Stepping delicately by his side, adorned in a sparkling gem-studded halter attached to a matching leash, was a tiny pig. John and Annie giggled at the sight.

Ignoring their snickers, Dan bowed deeply before the children. As he did, the little pig bent low on her front legs in a comical mimic of the human beside her. "Lady and gentleman," Dan announced regally, "may I introduce you to Leah, the world's most learned pig!" At the sound of her name, Leah looked up and snorted. She reared up on her back legs and performed a perfect pirouette, much to John and Annie's delight. They applauded enthusiastically.

"That's wonderful, Dan!" exclaimed Annie. "How did you teach her to do that?"

"Oh, that's just one of her tricks, Annie," Dan replied. "Would you like to see her tell time?" Both Annie and John nodded.

Dan addressed his piglet solemnly. "Now, Leah, we don't want to be late for our appearance in today's parade. Would you please be so kind as to tell me the time?" Stretching out his arm, Dan made a dramatic sweeping gesture toward the sunny sky. "Would you say twelve o'clock, Leah?" The pig shook her head back and forth, as if saying no. "Would you say eleven o'clock, Leah?" Again, the little pig shook her head. Finally, Dan asked firmly, "Leah, is it ten o'clock?" This time Leah snorted, and bobbed her head up and down, agreeing that indeed it was ten o'clock. The tinny chime of the small clock in Mary's wagon confirmed the accuracy of Leah's answer.

"That's amazing!" John said to Dan. "How did you teach her that?"

"That's my secret," Dan replied. "She has many other tricks as well. In fact, she'll be helping both of you today."

John was dumbfounded. "How will she do that?" he asked.

"When the time is right, I will give Leah the signal to run away from the parade," Dan explained. "When she does, you and Annie and I will chase her into the crowd where your next conductor will be waiting."

Annie and John looked uncertain. "Do you mean that we're supposed to follow a pig to our next stop?" Annie asked.

"That's right, Annie. But remember," Dan replied with a wink, "this is not just any pig. This is Leah, the world's most learned pig!" He picked up the squirming pink animal and started off toward the field where the wagons and animals were beginning to assemble for the parade.

Shaking their heads and mumbling to themselves in disbelief, Annie and John followed close at his heels, wondering what in the world would happen next!

All of the circus performers had gathered to organize the parade. Jack Fisher, dressed in blue trapeze attire complete with a long velvet cape, was addressing the crowd from atop a wagon. "May I have your attention, please?" he hollered, trying to quiet the noisy group. "Remember, your performance on the streets of Wickliffe this morning will surely determine our revenue this evening!" His audience nodded their heads in agreement. "Let's look lively out there! Make them want to see our show!"

Jack set about lining up the animals and performers. He motioned to Annie and John. "You two look wonderful!" he exclaimed. "Has Dan explained how Leah will lead you this morning?" When Annie and John nodded, Jack continued, "That's fine. Now let's get you in place." He led them to the front of the parade where Dan and Leah were waiting beside Josie.

In the morning sunshine, Sarah Josepha looked absolutely spectacular. On her head she wore a bejeweled harness that glimmered with sapphires and diamonds. The gems were just paste, Annie knew, but still they looked very authentic as they sparkled in the sun. Her broad back was covered with a silk cloth woven in an array of watery pastels. A large gold painted bench rested high on her back, held in place by braided leather straps that tied under her belly. A red satin cushion rested on the bench.

"Climb on up, Annie!" Jack ordered her.

"What?" Annie squeaked, stepping away from the animal.

"You'll have the best seat in the parade!" Dan told her. "Come on, and I'll show you how it's done."

Gingerly, Dan grabbed hold of Josie's trunk. As if on cue, Josie lifted her front leg for Dan to step on. From there it was an easy swing up to the bench. Dan waved down to her from his perch. "See!" he teased. "It's simple!"

Dan climbed gracefully down from the elephant's back, and offered his hand to Annie. "Up you go!" he said as he lifted her onto Josie's leg. From there Annie scrambled rather awkwardly up onto the bench. She tied herself in securely with a leather strap.

"I guess I'm ready," she called down, her uncertainty evident.

"Just hold on, and you'll be fine!" Jack assured her. Smiling at John, he said, "Your placement won't be nearly as exciting. You need to stay on this side of Josie. When Leah runs into the crowd, you must be ready to follow her."

Dan piped up. "When we get close to the docks, I'll help Annie get down, and then she and I will follow you. With your bad leg, you might need a little bit of a head start." John nodded, and Dan took his position with Leah. After a brief walk down a dirt road from the circus camp, the procession stopped at the end of Main Street. The Flying Fishers Circus and Exotic Menagerie was ready to begin its parade.

"Step off!" yelled Jack. Led by a half dozen musicians dressed in flamboyant purple and gold uniforms, the parade began its mile-long journey through the streets of Wickliffe. The performers and animals alike seemed to move in step with the quick cadence of the band music. Annie found herself bobbing to and fro with Josie's gentle swaying, and discovered to her surprise that riding an elephant was great fun!

Once the music began, the citizens of the town poured out of their doors to line the streets. Shopkeepers stood on their front stoops, brooms in hand, watching the performers. Mothers stopped their housecleaning and opened upstairs windows so that their babies could get a better view. Bigger boys and girls gathered along the edges of the roads, their mouths open in amazement, their hands clapping to the infectious beat of the circus band. Dogs barked, horses whinnied, and children and grown-ups alike laughed at the fantastic spectacle. It was a wonderful cacophony of sights and sounds, and Annie and John were enjoying it all!

Josie and Annie, following closely behind the band, drew loud cheers from the crowds. Behind the elegant elephant and her nervous rider, acrobats clad in tight silver costumes were doing flips and cartwheels. One of the men was walking on his hands while another did somersaults down the road. The acrobats were followed by a troupe of men and women who were dressed as giants in brightly colored pants and long, long dresses. They moved gracefully on tall stilts, but had to be careful not to lose their hats in the tree limbs.

Animal trainers came next. A group of little dogs, each wearing a huge ruffled collar, performed intricate jumps and flips. The wagon containing the kangaroo was close behind, and after that came the infamous and threatening "strangling serpent." Bringing up the rear was Bert, the Flying Fishers' own "unicorn." Frightened children clung to their mothers' skirts when he passed by, for they had never seen a beast like that before.

Up and down the road, jugglers entertained the crowd with their clever tricks, while clowns threw peanuts to the throngs of waiting children who grabbed up the dusty-shelled treats. Mary waved from the window of her wagon, her cheerful greetings making the audience smile.

Time passed quickly for both Annie and John, for soon Dan gave the signal that it was time for Annie to climb down. The parade was nearing the dock, and the crowd had thinned slightly. The circus would turn around here and return to the camp the way it had come. When the parade arrived back at the big tent, the show would begin, and the animals would be on display for anyone who wanted to pay to see them.

When Annie had both feet solidly on the ground, she heard Dan give Leah the command. "Go, Leah, go!" he whispered in her ear. The little piglet ran for all she was worth, with John, Annie, and Dan in hot pursuit.

"Leah! Leah!" Dan called out lamely as the pig disappeared down a backstreet. The young clowns pushed through the laughing crowd, with Dan making meager apologies as they went. The three made quite a sight: the silly white clown with the pointed hat, the old-fashioned lady clown in the purple dress, and the old man clown, limping along, each doing their best to catch the squealing little pig.

It wasn't long before Leah led the trio down a side street to the back of a vacant warehouse. She disappeared behind the building. Annie and John followed quickly behind, and were amazed at the sight that awaited them. Leah was there, resting comfortably in the arms of an old man that neither Annie nor John had ever seen before. The man was holding Leah in the crook of his arm, crooning to her and scratching the back of her ear. The piglet's head was thrown back in an expression of utter bliss.

"Annie and John, this is Captain Richardson," Dan puffed, out of breath from the long run. "He'll be taking you to your next stop."

"How do you do, children?" the sea captain asked. He gently returned Leah to Dan's waiting arms. "If you'll follow me," Thomas Richardson said, "I'll show you to your next mode of transport. From here to Quincy, Illinois, you'll be traveling on my steamship, *The Sinon*."

As Annie and John walked away with the captain, Dan called after them. "Wait! I have something for both of you!" He reached up under his sleeve and pulled out two bracelets. They were very simple, made of black fiber. "They're elephant hair," Dan explained. "They are made of hair that came from Josie's tail. Circus folk believe that they bring good luck." He smiled, and tied a bracelet on Annie's wrist, and then on John's.

"Thanks for everything, Dan," John said.

"I'll never forget you or Josie," Annie remarked, her eyes watering just a little. She hugged Dan gently, turning away when Captain Richardson called.

"Come, John and Annie! We must hurry! You still have quite a journey ahead of you!"

23

Stowaways

"Hide in here until the setting sun crosses this line on the wall," Captain Richardson explained to Annie and John. The trio was standing in the abandoned warehouse near the waterfront. Captain Richardson had shone them the little makeshift room that had been designed for use by his special passengers, the escaping slaves.

He was pointing to a black mark on the wall, barely a scuff on the wooden plank. "See here," he pointed, "when the sun is at just the right place in the sky, it will shine through that window yonder. The shadow of the bar there on the ledge should land right about there this time of year." He rubbed his hand over the mark, showing them what they were to look for. "You have only a couple of hours to wait. That will be your signal." The captain walked over to the door and pointed to some crates stacked near the dock. "Now, when I walk out of here, I'm going to head straight for those crates. I'll take out my handkerchief, pretend to blow my nose, and leave the cloth on the one that's empty. When no one is watching, get in that crate and close the top."

He looked at the young people, noting the fear on their faces. "Move quickly and quietly, and you've nothing to fear. It'll be almost nightfall by then, and the docks will be mostly deserted." He patted their shoulders, and smiled. "You won't be the first pair of stowaways that's gotten aboard my ship this way!"

Walking to the corner of the room, the captain pulled a canvas tarpaulin off some boxes. "There's food and water in here, and some blankets if you want to rest for a little while. Try to scrub off some of that clown makeup if you can. I'm sorry I don't have other clothes for you, but we'll take care of that as soon as we can. Just remember to keep your eye on that wall!" He turned toward the door as he started to leave.

"Captain," John asked, making the captain look back, "what do we do once we're on board the ship?"

"Stay hidden in the crate. I'll come down to the hold as soon as we're under way to show you the special 'stateroom' that I have ready for you!" Captain Richardson chuckled, and the children smiled. With a wave of his hand, the captain was gone.

Peeking through the slats of the old wooden door, John watched as Captain Richardson walked to one of the crates. He saw the man double over in an exaggerated fit of sneezing, pull out his handkerchief, and blow his nose. As he tried to stuff the cloth back into his pocket, it "accidentally" fell on a nearby crate.

"That must be the one!" John whispered, smiling. He pointed out the empty container to Annie. The two children went back to the corner, and cleaned their faces and hands with the water the captain had provided. After some food and a little rest, they would be ready for the next part of their dangerous journey.

* * *

Abraham had concluded his business for Clayton's client and was back on the ship by supper time. It had been an easy job, Abraham had to admit, and the dollars he'd earned would certainly fatten his pocket.

After a rather unappetizing meal, he decided a brief walk on the deck would help clear his head and, perhaps, settle his stomach. *Too many meals on this ship could be deadly for either man or beast, he concluded. I do miss Miriam's home cooking!*

Leaning over the rail of the steamship, Abraham studied the little town of Wickliffe as it readied itself for the night. Lights were being extinguished in the few shops that lined the main road.

Candles and oil lamps flickered in the windows of homes that would soon be warm and cozy as families came together to share their suppers. Smoke from a dozen chimneys spiraled into the darkening sky, wispy and black against the colorful pallet of the winter sunset. Looking to the east, Abraham saw ominous storm clouds forming, their silhouettes mixing with the approaching night.

Off in the distance Abraham could see the bright circus lanterns, sprinkled like glowing fireflies on the outskirts of town. He had watched some of the Flying Fishers circus parade that afternoon, and had been intrigued by the marvelous elephant. He had laughed with the townspeople as three clowns had unsuccessfully chased a pig down the street, so obviously outwitted were they by the animal's clever maneuvers. He smiled at the recollection.

His gaze had moved from the countryside to the wharf when suddenly Abraham noticed two human shadows, ghostlike, moving on the dock among the crates that were about to be loaded on to *The Sinon*. When the workers drew close to them, the small shadows knelt down, hidden in the darkening twilight. As the workers moved away, hauling heavy loads up the gang plank, Abraham saw the shadows again. This time, he watched as one shadow pried up the lid of a nearby crate. Both specters hurriedly climbed inside, pulling the lid back over the top to hide themselves. Just as they were completely hidden from view, two of the crew members bent to pick up the dubious box, grunting in frustration at the heaviness of their load. Their well-chosen and colorful curses drifted to Abraham's ears, and tickled his funny bone. But lift they did, and within a few minutes the crate was loaded into the hold of the waiting steamship.

"Hmmm," Abraham murmured. "A couple of young stowaways. This voyage is about to get even more interesting!"

Making his way toward the wheelhouse, Abraham could see Captain Richardson busily preparing to get under way. Abraham tapped on the door to get the captain's attention, but the man waved him off good-naturedly. "I'll be with you in a few minutes,

Abraham!" he called through the window, and turning away he continued barking orders at his officers.

With a shrug, Abraham walked toward the stairway that lead below to the hold. "I suppose I'll just have to do some investigating myself," he muttered aloud. He heard the steamer's paddle wheel as it began its rhythmic beating of the river waters. He felt the ship lurch forward just as he reached the lower decks of *The Sinon.*

Abraham's vision was obscured by the almost total blackness of the ship's hold. He scolded himself for neglecting to bring a lantern, and turned to go back up the steps when a noise from the stacks of crates caused him to freeze in his tracks. "Hello?" he hollered into the darkness. "I know you're there. Come on out where I can see you." He waited for a reply, but got none. "Fine, then," Abraham called. "I'll be back in a few minutes with the captain. He's not going to take lightly to stowaways aboard his ship!"

Abraham climbed slowly up the steps, listening for any sound below. At the top, he sat down on the step and waited patiently for the stowaways to make their move. His patience was rewarded when he heard voices coming from the cargo hold.

"Annie, we can't get out until the captain comes. He told us to stay in the crate." Abraham heard a small voice whisper. "Here, I'll open the lid just a little so that we have some more air."

Abraham heard the sliding of wood against wood. He waited.

"Thank you, John," whispered another voice.

Are those children's voices I hear? He wondered, surprised. Why would children be hiding aboard this ship? What's going on here?

Standing up, Abraham turned to go in search of the captain. He had taken only a few steps when he ran headlong into Thomas Richardson, coming through a passageway, a lantern in his hand.

"Captain, you must come with me," Abraham said urgently. "There is something in the lower deck that you must see." The lawyer walked quickly down the stairs, the captain following on his heels.

145

"Abraham, if this is about the stowaways," the captain said in a low voice. "I already know about them."

"What?" Abraham asked. "You know that there are stowaways aboard?

They were at the bottom of the stairs now, and both men stopped. Captain Richardson called out, "Annie! John! You may come out now. No one is here to see but our friend Abraham Lincoln, and he won't hurt you, will you, Abraham?" In the glow of the captain's lamp, Abraham saw him smiling.

Out of one of the crates scrambled two small bodies, both in odd costumes and strange head coverings. In the dim light, Abraham could just make out faint traces of white paint on the otherwise dark faces of the boy and girl.

"The clowns!" Abraham exclaimed. "You're two of the clowns that were chasing that ridiculous pig! What are you doing here?"

Captain Richardson put his arms around John and Annie. "Abraham, I can't answer your questions right now. You'll just have to trust me. I'll have to ask you to keep our secret, too, at least for a time. Can you do that?"

When Abraham nodded mutely, the captain continued. "Then will you excuse us for a time while I get Annie and John settled? We'll talk later, I promise."

Abraham watched as Captain Richardson shepherded his stowaways to the back of the hold. Then he made his way up the stairs and out on to the deck. Surprised by the cold rain that pelted his face as he reached the top of the stairs, Abraham made a beeline to his stateroom. For tonight he'd have to content himself with his books. He realized that he'd get no answers for his questions until the captain was ready to give them.

Down below in the hold, the captain was helping to settle his two young guests in their quarters. A small, narrow room had been constructed across the back of the deck. Its tiny entrance was hidden by an old rotted canvas that hung like a curtain across the wall. Strange wooden planks, as tall and as wide as a man, were laid side by side across the false wall, further obscuring the appearance of the room.

"A little room, just like at the Thompsons!" Annie remarked.

"What are these planks used for?" John asked the captain. He noted the two slits in the boards, both located right where a man's shoulders might be.

"Oh, John," the captain replied. "These are life preservers. Should the crew ever have to abandon ship, they can grab one of these." Picking up a board, he stood it in front of John. "A man could secure his arms through these slits, like this," he explained, pulling the boy's arms through the holes. "The wood will float in the water, of course, and the man would be able to paddle himself to safety."

John clasped his hands together on the other side of the wood, and nodded his approval. "Let's hope we don't have to try this out too soon!" John said as the sound of waves pounding the ship could be heard through the hull.

"We're in for a little rough weather tonight," the captain said, "but I wouldn't worry about it. *The Sinon* has weathered many a nasty storm in her day!"

Leaving his lantern in the room with John and Annie, Captain Richardson told the children to put out the light as soon as they were settled, and he would see them in the morning.

"Good night, Captain!" Annie and John whispered. The rocking of the ship lulled the children to sleep even as the storm worsened.

24

Athwart Hawse!

The driving rains and blackness of the night, as impenetrable as onyx, made navigating the Mississippi particularly difficult. More than once, Thomas considered heading to shore to wait out the storm. He knew the precious human cargo hidden below couldn't wait, however, and so he pushed on, keeping as close to the riverbanks as possible.

About midnight, *The Sinon* approached a bend in the river. Because his vessel was heading upstream, Captain Richardson knew that he was expected to cross his ship to the far banks where the water moved slowest. Ships heading downstream would be following the channel out toward the middle where the water ran the fastest. Thomas did not relish the idea of steering *The Sinon* across the wild river, but he knew that laws of navigation required this of him.

"Keep a close eye out, Mr. Masters!" the captain hollered to his lookout.

"Aye, sir!" the man replied, his answer all but washed away in the storm.

* * *

Several miles upstream, near the town of Pelican Point, a huge barge loaded with barrels and crates of all sizes and descriptions was straining at its moorings in the fearsome storm. The dock pilings ached and the heavy ropes groaned with effort as they struggled to hold the heavy barge in place. Finally, the Mississippi had her way, and with a mighty pull of the raging waters, the vessel broke free.

It careened toward the center of the channel where the currents dragged it faster and faster downstream. Hurtling out of control, it rushed down the frenzied river, straight into the path of *The Sinon*.

* * *

"Athwart hawse!" yelled Captain Richardson above the screaming of the storm and the splintering of wood as the two vessels collided. "She's sheared off our bow! Abandon ship!"

Abraham awoke to the ship's bells clanging in the darkness. He could barely hear the yelling of the crew above the fury of the wind, but he realized immediately that something was terribly wrong.

Struggling into his clothes, he threw open the door to his stateroom and ran out onto the deck. Below him men were running helter-skelter as they tried to secure the ill-fated ship. In the raging waters of the river he could make out a dozen or so of the crew, clinging frantically to crates, barrels, and whatever other flotsam might keep them afloat.

Suddenly Thomas was standing beside him, soaked to the skin, a grim expression on his face. "Can you swim, Abraham?" he yelled in the man's ear. When Abraham nodded, the captain continued, "Get the children. You're the only man I can trust. Get them to shore, if you can. May God go with you! Go, now!" Without waiting for Abraham's reply, the captain turned on his heel and ran down the deck of his doomed vessel, hollering out orders that Thomas prayed would save his men's lives.

Abraham pushed his way down the steps to the main deck. The enormous barge had settled itself across the front of the ship, and a huge fire had erupted. Men were scrambling to salvage whatever they could of the cargo, even as their captain ordered them to abandon ship. When Abraham got to the hold he found it already knee-deep in water, and tilting dangerously to starboard.

"Annie! John!" he yelled. "It's Abraham! I'm here to help you! Where are you?"

Light from the fire on deck helped to illuminate the hold, and Abraham watched as two quavering shadows emerged from beneath a soaked canvas.

"Can either of you swim?" Abraham asked. John nodded, but Annie shook her head, her eyes filled with terror.

"I never learned, Mr. Abraham," she replied tearfully.

"It's all right, Annie," John told her. "Look, we'll use these." Grabbing one of the life preservers that Thomas had shown him, John pulled Annie's arms through the slits. Now there was only one board left by the panicked crew, and John quickly handed it to Abraham.

The older man smiled. "I admire your courage," Abraham told him, "but I'm a fair swimmer myself. My job is to get you to safety." Handing the board back to the boy, he steered the two up the steps to the deck.

Heading away from the fire, Abraham led the children aft, to the back railing. He noticed that the rain had diminished somewhat and the wind had calmed, but the boat was listing at a deadly angle. He feared that *The Sinon* would be gone within a matter of minutes.

"We're going to have to jump, children," Abraham said with more calm than he felt. "We'll try to stay together, but if we are separated, head there, toward that rock on the shore."

Realizing that there was no other alternative the youngsters nodded, and together the three jumped into the roiling river. Currents soon drove them apart. Within seconds, Annie was screaming as the waves churned about her, flipping over the life preserver and dumping her into the frigid water.

A strong swimmer, John was able to navigate the currents, and he came to rest in the shallows by the rock. Seeing that the boy was safe, Abraham began to make his way toward Annie.

With broad strokes, he fought through the swells, struggling with all his might to reach the panicked girl. Pausing, he lifted his head and looked all about for her, but she had disappeared beneath the black water. Frantically he called out to her but got no response.

"John, do you see her?" he yelled to the boy onshore.

John scanned the water's surface, looking for his friend. "Yes, she's there!" he hollered, pointing to an outcropping of rocks twenty yards downstream from Abraham. In an odd twist of fate, the deadly fire aboard *The Sinon* was now serving as a beacon of light on the waterway, making Annie's arms visible as they flailed about in the water. The wooden board had been destroyed when it crashed on the rocks. Only broken planks remained, bobbing about uselessly in the waves.

Letting the currents carry him, Abraham swam quickly to the girl. He knew at once that she was trapped, her foot wedged in the rocks below the surface of the chest-deep water. She was struggling for air, her head held just inches above the river. Diving down, Abraham could hardly see in the murky water. Feeling his way in the icy depths, he grabbed hold of her leg. He tugged but could not pull her free.

Coming to the surface, he saw that John was already there in the water with them. The boy hurriedly pushed Annie's shoulders up, allowing her to inhale precious breaths of air. Abraham dove back down into the freezing water. Again he took hold of her leg and pulled. This time he felt the foot give way, and the girl was free.

Wrapping his arms around her thin body, Abraham dragged Annie to the shore. John followed, trudging through the shallows, soaked and exhausted. Shivering in the cold, they collapsed on the wet banks, trying to catch their breaths.

"Thank you, Mr. Abraham," was all Annie could say as she gasped for air.

Another explosion on the deck of *The Sinon* shook the riverbank, sending bright flames high into the night sky. The trio watched in horror as, within seconds, the steamship slipped beneath the water, disappearing into the depths.

Several hundred yards upstream, Abraham watched as crew members straggled to the shore, falling on their faces in the mud of the Mississippi shoreline. Those to arrive first had already started small fires on the banks to warm themselves. The flames cast dancing lights on the river, illuminating the shores. Abraham was relieved to see the silhouette of his friend, Thomas Richardson, standing knee-deep in the shallows, helping to pull his men from the water.

With a deep sigh, he turned to his young friends. "Let's get one of those fires going ourselves," Abraham said. "We could use a little warmth to get these clothes dry." For the first time he noticed that the children had exchanged their clown costumes for more practical attire: long-sleeved muslin shirts and overalls, even for Annie.

Seeing the question in his eyes, Annie laughed. "I must look quite a sight to you, Mr. Abraham, but this outfit suits the life of a runaway slave much better than a lavender lace dress. Don't you think?"

Abraham nodded, but then commented, "That lavender dress might have been the death of you. I'm not sure I could have gotten you out of the water if that had gotten tangled up in those rocks. As it was, it took both me and John to rescue you!"

Patting John on the back, Abraham said, "You're quite a brave young man. Annie and I are both lucky to have you along."

Annie murmured shyly, "He's right, John. Thank you." She kissed him lightly on the cheek, and John smiled broadly.

"Well, now, ain't this sweet?" a familiar voice crooned sarcastically.

Wheeling around, Abraham, Annie, and John watched in disbelief as Willie Hall and his lackey, Davey, rode their horses down the riverbank. Davey's gun lay casually across his saddle, sending an unspoken warning. "If it ain't that stupid lawyer, Abraham Lincoln!" Willie sniggered. "And with him is the sister of the dumbest black boy I ever did meet! How are you doing, Annie?"

Furious, Annie lunged at the man, battering him with her fists. Willie reached down from his saddle, and slapped her away, knocking her to the ground. Angrily, Abraham and John started toward Willie with their fists raised, but Davey aimed his gun in their direction, stopping them dead in their tracks.

"What are you doing here, Willie?" Abraham demanded, enraged by the man's actions. "I thought you were well on your way south. Did you just stay around here to pick on young girls?"

"Now there's no need for anyone to get hurt, Abraham," Willie said condescendingly. "You and the boy here need to calm down." Looking appraisingly at John, Willie asked, "Just what are you anyway, boy? You're one of those lousy Cherokees moving out to the Oklahoma Territory, aren't you? I've seen 'em camped out on the other side of the river."

With a malicious grin, he turned to his partner. "It looks like we've just doubled our earnings on this little trip, Davey. We'll collect a nice reward for the girl, being as she's a runaway slave. Then we'll collect a reward from the United States government for the boy since he's a runaway, too." While Davey kept his gun pointed squarely at Abraham and the children, Willie climbed down from his horse. Pulling some rope from his saddlebag, he moved first to tie up Abraham.

"Now wait just a minute, Willie," the lawyer said. "Perhaps we can work out a trade. Would ten dollars in gold make any difference to you?"

A wide grin broke out on the horse thief's whiskered face. "Well now, Abraham Lincoln, we might just be able to make a deal after all!"

25

Honest Abe

John squeezed Abraham's hand hard. He'd heard a sound in the woods behind the two horse thieves, and he was trying to warn Abraham. There was no need for this; the older man had heard the noise as well, and had an inkling of what was making it. He was busily trying to distract Willie and Davey with a conversation about their favorite subject: gold.

"Let us go, Willie, and you can have my money. Neither one of these two runaways is going to be worth very much. Besides, it'll be a lot of trouble to collect the rewards." Abraham's training as a lawyer was serving him well. His words were designed to distract the two hoodlums, giving his rescuer time to make his move.

"And what's to keep me from taking the money anyway, along with the girl and boy? Are you going to stop me?" Willie asked smugly. Davey was beside him now, his gun pointed directly at Abraham's heart.

"Maybe he won't, but I certainly will!" yelled Thomas Richardson, coming up behind Davey and knocking the weapon from his hand. With one good hard fist to the jaw, Davey crumpled unconscious into the mud.

Abraham took the opportunity to make short work of Willie Hall. Relying on the wrestling moves he became famous for as a youth, Abraham used a well-placed head butt to drop his opponent to the ground, pinning him there, Willie's face in the mud. Grinning, Thomas shoved a handkerchief in Willie's mouth to keep him quiet. Then he handed Abraham a length of rope to tie him up.

Annie and John stood staring in amazement. "Where did you learn to do that?" John asked, looking from Abraham to Willie and then back again.

"I used to wrestle some as a lad," Abraham replied modestly. "I guess there are some things that you just never forget!"

Thomas had finished tying Davey's hands behind his back, and was now busily securing his legs. "This one won't be going anywhere for awhile," Thomas remarked. "I'll get a couple of my men to come down here and clean up this little mess of ours. They'll make sure that Willie and Davey are properly introduced to the local sheriff!

"Take their two horses, Abraham. By my reckoning, you should be about two days' ride due north to Springfield. I'll meet up with you there as soon as I can."

Hearing this, Willie began to writhe and moan. He shook his head violently, his eyes wide with anger. The gag in his mouth made speech impossible.

"What's wrong with you?" Thomas demanded, pulling the rag from the horse thief's mouth. "You got something to say that's worth hearing?"

Willie grimaced, spitting bits of dirt and cotton thread onto the ground. "Don't take them horses," he begged. "They're the only ones Davey and I ever bought fair and square!" He looked pleadingly at Thomas and Abraham, who stood smiling at the irony of Willie's situation.

"Here you go, Willie," Abraham said, tossing a little sack of gold coins at the man's feet. "This is payment for the horses. I've never cheated anyone out of their goods or money, and I'm not about to start now."

For the second time tonight, John and Annie stood staring at their friend in amazement. "After all the troubles he's caused us,

Abraham?" Annie asked, shivering now in her wet clothes and cold winter wind.

Abraham took a blanket from Davey's horse and wrapped it around Annie's shoulders. "I'll never let myself be like Willie," Abraham told her. "If I took these horses, I'd be just like him, a common horse thief. That's not how I want to live my life. Do you?"

Annie shook her head. "No, I guess not." She snuggled deeper into the blanket, thankful for its warmth. When she moved closer to the fire, she could see the intricate patterns of the quilt, its precise stitches forming familiar lines across the soft cloth.

With a burst of recognition, Annie felt tears form in her eyes and anger burn in her heart. "Where did you get this blanket?" she cried, kicking wildly at Willie who sat on the ground with his back propped against an oak tree. "This is my mother's quilt!" she screamed, while Willie, in a panic, scrambled to avoid her flying feet. John grabbed her arms, and pulled her back.

"Davey must have taken it from your brother," Willie sputtered, struggling to get away from the enraged girl. "I didn't take it! Stop kicking me!" he shrieked.

Wrapping his long arms around her comfortingly, Abraham spoke to the girl softly. "Annie, we'll keep the blanket now. You'll be able to give it back to your mother when you're all together in Springfield," Abraham said soothingly. "It will be a wonderful surprise for her!" Abraham's gentle words worked their magic, and Annie calmed down.

With a scowl on his whiskered face, Thomas took the dirty rag and shoved it back into Willie's mouth. "We've heard enough from you. You can tell the rest of your story to the sheriff."

John had taken a brief inventory of the supplies that Willie and Davey had stored in their saddlebags. "We should have plenty of food to keep us going for several days. And these horses," he continued grinning, cutting his eyes at the furious Willie, "will make fine mounts for a 'stupid lawyer,' a 'lousy Cherokee runaway,' and 'the sister of the dumbest black boy' Willie Hall ever met!"

Thomas, Abraham, and Annie all laughed at that, but Willie just scowled. Abraham mounted the tall mare, her white-stockinged legs long and graceful, her delicate head adorned with a white star set between two large gentle eyes. He motioned for Annie to join him, and Thomas helped her up. John climbed into the saddle of Davey's horse, a sturdy coffee-colored Morgan that was snorting and pawing the ground impatiently.

"Remember, head due north, and that should bring you into Springfield in a couple of days. With any luck we've seen the worst of this nasty weather, and you'll have smooth sailing from here on!" Thomas said, shaking Abraham's hand.

"I'll see you in Springfield then, at the Widow Hall's," Abraham said, and in a low voice he added, "and you better have some answers for me!"

Grinning, Thomas just nodded his head, and slapped the rump of the mare. She took off at an even trot, and John's horse fell in line close behind. Annie and John both turned to wave farewell to the captain. Thomas smiled broadly, and waved his cap in a goodbye salute.

"You know, Mr. Abraham," Annie said as she leaned back comfortably against the man's chest, "Captain Richardson looks mighty handsome with that beard of his. You might want to think about growing one of your own. I mean, it would cover up that long white face of yours." Her voice trailed off as she realized how rude her suggestion must sound. Pressed securely against his chest, she could feel Abraham's muscles tighten, and his breathing catch.

In the awkward silence that followed, Annie was afraid that her bold words had insulted her friend. She couldn't believe that she'd been so blunt and unkind to this gentle man! An apology slowly took shape in her mind, but before she could get it out, she felt the beginning of laughter, rippling like river currents deep within Abraham's chest. The ripples multiplied, growing stronger

and stronger against her spine until, finally, one long rolling guf-
faw burst from his mouth, the joy of it echoing in the trees and
lighting up the dark, starless night.

"Well, Annie," he gasped in between snatches of laughter, "I'll
definitely ponder your suggestion." Annie heard John chuckle in
the darkness.

The three rode on together amiably, through a splendid sunrise and straight into a warm afternoon. They followed a well-
used game trail that Abraham correctly discerned was heading in a
northerly direction. It meandered along a small creek that provided
the riders and horses with fresh water. At dusk they came upon an
old cabin, decayed and decrepit, but welcome shelter nonetheless.
They climbed down from the weary horses, and stood studying the
crumbling structure.

A pair of enormous black walnut trees flanked the sides of the
rotting building like two ancient arms, stretching up gnarled fin-
gerlike branches from the forest floor. The wooden door of the
cabin blew open and closed at the whim of the wind, like the tooth-
less mouth of a sleeping old woman, lost in dreams of her youth.
Vines and branches, barren of greenery in the cold Illinois winter,
had woven themselves through the splintered wall boards, and hung
like wild eyebrows over the bare windows that stared menacingly
at the visitors.

"At least we'll sleep out of the weather tonight," Abraham
commented cheerfully. "It's not much to look at, but for now, it's
home!" Carefully he climbed the three broken steps that led to a
broad front porch whose planks sagged beneath his heavy boots.
The children followed warily behind him.

The cabin's interior was nearly as decayed as its exterior. A
lifeless hornets' nest hung suspended from a wooden beam in the
corner of the little room, its papery gray form, egg-shaped, was
barely visible in the slanted evening light. Various animal drop-
pings littered the filthy floor. A legless wooden chair squatted by
the fireplace, waiting its turn to be burned as kindling. Thick, ropy

cobwebs draped the room like party festoons gone awry.

"Miriam Hall would say that you could throw a cat through the gaps in these boards!" Abraham exclaimed as he put his entire fist through a hole between the rough-hewn planks that comprised the walls. Moving to the fireplace, he easily broke apart the old chair and tossed the pieces of wood onto the grate. It took John seconds with his flint to have a small fire burning brightly, its light and warmth welcome additions to the cold, dark room.

"We'll need more wood for the fire to get us through the night," Abraham told the children. "Annie, go through the saddlebags and see what you can muster up for dinner. John, would you help me gather some wood? It will take both of us to collect enough."

John followed Abraham outside, pausing at one of the black walnut trees. His eyes traveled from the tree to the small pond that had formed in a bend of the river behind the cabin. "Mr. Abraham," he said, rubbing his hand thoughtfully over the coarse, rough bark of the tree, "maybe you'd rather have some fresh fish for dinner?"

"That would be a welcome treat, John, but we have no hooks or lines. How do you propose we catch that fresh fish?"

Smiling, John took out his knife and began to shave pieces of bark from the walnut tree. He carried the bark to the back of the cabin, where the stream fed a small pond. Putting the bark on a flat rock, he knelt on the muddy shore of the pond and selected a rock about the size of his hand. Using the rock, he pounded the bark. In a short time the bark had been pulverized to a powder.

"Now watch this, Mr. Abraham," John said, rising to his feet and gathering the powder in his hands. He walked around the pond, Abraham close at his heels. Several fish as long as John's arm from elbow to wrist, flashed iridescent in the shallow water. They were silvery gray with a broad red band along their sides.

"A couple of nice looking trout there, John," Abraham commented. "But how do you propose to catch them with a handful of bark dust?"

"An old Cherokee trick," John replied with a grin, but then his face grew serious. Whispering in the ancient tongue of The People, John spoke what Abraham could only assume was a prayer. When John finished, he tossed the powdered bark into the pond where the fish were swimming.

Within a few minutes, two of the trout floated motionless to the top. Abraham watched as John stepped into the water, placed his hands under the immobile fish, and tossed them onto the bank at Abraham's feet.

Bending down to examine the fish, Abraham cried out, "John, these trout are completely stupefied! They're not dead, just unconscious!" Taking off his jacket, Abraham wrapped up the unmoving fish and looked admiringly at the young Cherokee lad. "If I hadn't seen it with my own eyes, I probably wouldn't have believed it. I'll never forget that little trick of your people, John!"

All that Annie had found left in the saddlebags was the same tough jerky that Mr. Smith had been so fond of. Her empty stomach growled at the thought of settling for that again. "It's better than going hungry, I guess," she said. She sat down by the small fire, rubbing her hands together for warmth, and waited for John and Abraham to return.

She heard laughter in their voices as they came up the porch steps. "Annie!" Abraham called out. "Wait until you see what John has caught for our dinner!"

Annie jumped up and ran to the door. Abraham proudly held out the two trout, his face beaming. John followed close behind, his arms full of wood for the fire.

"We'll have a feast tonight!" Annie crowed.

"And tomorrow night, we'll be home!" shouted Abraham.

26

A Cord of Three Strands

The captain and the lawyer were seated in the Widow Hall's parlor on the first warm spring day in early March. Sunlight filtered through the glass-paned windows and lit the cozy room with an amber glow. Miriam's delicious cookies and fragrant tea had put the two men in a mellow mood as they sat enjoying each other's company.

"For a man with such obvious intelligence, you demonstrate an unusual lack of curiosity, Abraham," the jovial captain remarked. "You never asked me about the name of my stalwart vessel. Haven't you wondered what The Sinon means?"

Abraham leaned back against the upholstered settee, his long legs stretched out in front of him. "Honestly, Captain," he replied sheepishly, "I never gave it much thought. But come to think of it, that is an unusual name. I'll wager the ancient Greeks are involved in it somehow!"

Captain Richardson settled himself comfortably in the generously cushioned chair across from Abraham, and began to relate the story. "The Greeks were having a war with the people of Troy, over a woman of course." His eyes sparkled. "The war had gone on for nine years, and the Greeks had enjoyed little success. The great city of Troy was surrounded by a wall that no army could penetrate by ordinary means. Finally, one of their favored sons, clever Odysseus, ordered that a huge wooden horse be constructed."

Captain Richardson paused, taking a sip of his cinnamon tea.

Abraham smiled patiently, waiting for the man to continue.

"The horse was enormous but hollow inside so that it could be filled with Greek soldiers. The Greeks made a big show of leaving the horse as a gift for the Trojans, acknowledging the victory of the citizens of Troy and the defeat of the Greeks."

Abraham interrupted, "But when they took it inside the city walls, the Greek soldiers came pouring out and they subdued the Trojans! An excellent plan!"

Captain Richardson nodded. "However, it wasn't quite that simple. The Trojans didn't trust the Greeks, and were not immediately willing to allow the huge horse into their city. Knowing their enemy well by now, the Greeks anticipated this and left behind a man named Sinon."

"The name of your ship," Abraham remarked, thoroughly engrossed in the captain's tale.

"Correct. Sinon's job was to make the Trojans think that he was angry at his countrymen for leaving him behind. He was to act as a spy, and convince the enemy that the huge horse really was the innocent gift it appeared to be."

The captain placed his tea cup on the table, and leaned forward, resting his elbows on his knees. "The Trojans believed Sinon, and allowed the horse to be brought into the city. The soldiers were secretly smuggled into Troy, stormed out of the wooden horse, and finally defeated their enemy. It was a glorious victory for Greece!"

Looking squarely in Abraham's eyes, the captain said, "Now I'm known as Sinon, Abraham. My job has been to appear to be just another steamship captain transporting goods and passengers up and down the Mississippi. But in truth, I'm a conductor for the Underground Railroad. I'm carrying human cargo just like that Trojan horse did thousands of years ago." He smiled broadly as Abraham's jaw dropped.

"I never knew," the young man said, shaking his head in disbelief. "I didn't even suspect!"

"I'm good at my job!" Captain Richardson boasted good-humoredly. "I've been doing this for many years, and I have a wonderful accomplice."

At that moment, the parlor door slid opened and Miriam entered carrying a tray of cookies. She set the tray on the table, and then stepped behind the captain's chair. Her hand rested lightly on the captain's shoulder as she smiled at Lincoln. "I'm the accomplice, Abraham. Thomas and I have worked together as conductors for a long time now, and we've helped dozens of escaping slaves on their way to freedom. Remember when you helped me paint this house black and white? You thought that I'd lost my mind!" she laughed at the memory. "Those are the colors used by stations on the Underground Railroad. I wanted fleeing slaves to know that they'd find safety here."

Dumbfounded by this news, Abraham could only stare at the smiling couple. Thomas patted the woman's hand affectionately. "But now we're about to make this partnership official," he said, grinning. "We're going to be married on Sunday, and we'd like for you to be there as our witness. What do you say, Abraham?"

Coming to his senses, the lawyer finally spoke up. "Married? That's wonderful news! I'll be happy to stand up with you, Thomas!" Leaping to his feet, he crossed the room to where his landlady stood, and swept her up into his arms. "Best wishes for a wonderful life, Miriam!" he cried as he danced her around the parlor. Putting her down gently, he extended his hand to Thomas. "And congratulations to the groom!" his voice resounded joyfully. "What a wedding this will be!"

* * *

The following Sunday was as warm and bright as any spring day that Abraham could remember. It was perfect for a wedding, with crocuses blooming in gardens, and returning robins singing their welcome-home songs so that all could hear. Abraham could not be sure which was shining more vividly: the cheery March sun shining through puffy cotton clouds, or the beaming faces of

Thomas and Miriam, as they walked up the steps to the little white clapboard church.

John and Annie were already inside the chapel. They had been up since early that morning, gathering wildflowers to tie on the ends of the dozen wooden pews that faced the front of the sanctuary. On the altar, a glass vase held more flowers, and Annie handed Miriam a little nosegay of fresh blooms tied with pink and yellow ribbons.

"Thank you, Annie!" Miriam exclaimed. "Look how they match my dress!" Miriam did a little twirl for Annie, proudly showing off her best Sunday frock. Annie could not help but smile at the glowing bride-to-be.

The minister waited at the altar as the couple made their way down the center aisle of the church. John had practiced a new song on his flute, just for this occasion. He played the beautiful melody for Miriam and Thomas in honor of their wedding, and they smiled at him in appreciation. When John finished, he and Annie sat down on the front pew. Abraham, tall and lean in his best dark suit, stood proudly next to Thomas, handsome in his captain's uniform.

Thomas turned to face his bride. "To begin, Miriam, I've asked Abraham to read a passage from the Bible that is very meaningful to me. Abraham?"

Opening his well-worn Bible to the Old Testament, Abraham began to read the ancient words printed before him on the onion-thin page. "Ecclesiastes chapter 4, verses 9 through 12," he said, clearing his throat as he read the passage aloud to the tiny group.

Two are better than one,
Because they have a good return for their work:
If one falls down, his friend can help him up.
But pity the man who falls and has no one to help him up!
Also, if two lie down together, they will keep warm.
But how can one keep warm alone?
Though one may be overpowered, two can defend themselves.
A cord of three strands is not quickly broken.

Smiling, Abraham closed the book, and laid it on the bench behind him. Thomas turned to his bride again, speaking clearly so that everyone could hear. "Together we have accomplished much for freedom, Miriam. Now, with God's help as the third strand in this wonderful cord we've made, we can do even greater things." Taking Miriam's hands in his, he said gently, "Our work to end the misery of slavery has only begun. There is much more for us to do. Will you work with me as my partner and wife as we continue this labor that God has given us?"

Nodding her head, Miriam smiled lovingly at Thomas. "I will," she said.

"Then, let's get this ceremony started!" the minister's voice boomed in the little chapel. "Dearly beloved," he began.

Suddenly, the large church doors burst open, and a small boy flew down the center aisle. All heads turned to watch as Jacob threw his arms around Annie's neck.

"Jacob! You're here!" she shrieked with delight as she hugged him close. Then, looking past her little brother, she spied Isaiah walking toward her, a broad smile lighting his face.

"Isaiah!" she cried. Leaping to her feet, Annie threw herself into her brother's wide embrace. Laughing, Isaiah swung her off her feet and spun her around and around. Annie finally grew serious, her expression questioning.

"Mama? Papa? Are they with you?" she asked Isaiah, searching his eyes for the happy answer she wanted so desperately. Her brother lowered her gently to the floor.

Placing his strong hands firmly on her shoulders, he answered her. "They're not with us, Annie," he replied. "When the slave catchers took them back to the plantation, Papa was beaten terribly by Master Ellidge. Even after all these months, he's still healing, and Mama has to care for him. She sent me with Jacob. She and Papa want us to go on without them."

The happiness that had filled Annie's heart vanished as quickly as it had come. Fear took its place, as heavy as a huge boulder, crushing her chest. Tears threatened to spill from her eyes, but Isaiah drew her to him and wrapped his arms around her.

"Annie," he whispered, "when Papa gets well, they will come. They will find a way, and we will be together again." He smiled into her eyes, and Annie nodded.

"Annie!" an impatient Jacob hollered as he wiggled his way between his big brother and sister, "I'm hungry, hungry, hungry!" He pulled impatiently at her skirts, and Annie laughed.

They were not the only surprise guests at the wedding. Walking quietly down the aisle behind Annie's family were Charles and Susannah Thompson. Grinning from ear to ear, John ran to embrace his friends. Tears and smiles combined on the faces of the families reunited, as love and laughter filled up the little room. Abraham thought that he had never before witnessed such expressions of pure joy on human faces.

It was the minister who was finally able to bring some order to the cheerful chaos. "If all of our guests would be seated, we will continue with this wedding," he crowed. "And then we'll get this hungry young man some supper!" Jacob smiled.

When the vows were finished and the rings exchanged, Mr. and Mrs. Thomas Richardson led all of their wedding guests back to the boarding house where a feast awaited them.

Extra chairs were brought into the large dining room, and additional place settings laid for the unexpected guests. Annie could not wait another minute to hear about her family's journey.

"How did you do this, Isaiah? How did you get here?" Biscuit crumbs flew from her mouth as she spoke. Miriam handed her a napkin which Annie quickly brushed across her mouth.

"Well," Isaiah began slowly, obviously enjoying the attention of everyone at the table. "It was a long walk to Alabama. When I finally got back to the plantation, Miss Becca helped me get a message to Mama and Papa. She risked her life to help me get Jacob off the plantation," Isaiah said seriously.

"She got word to our old friend, 'Mr. Smith,' that we needed help, and Jacob and I made the journey back to the Thompson farm.

"Turned out that Charles and Susannah were making plans to come up this way to Illinois to see you, John," Isaiah grinned at his friend. "So, we just tagged along with them."

"He became quite an actor," Charles beamed at Isaiah. "Since *The Sinon* was no longer available, we had to secure passage on one of your sister ships, Thomas. Isaiah became our servant boy, and Jacob was his little helper." Jacob smiled at the mention of his name, and milk dribbled down his chin.

Charles laughed. "Susannah got very accustomed to having him wait on her hand and foot. I'm not sure what I'm going to do with her now. She's become quite the princess!"

"Charles! That's not true!" Susannah exclaimed, her face blushing crimson with indignation. After a moment she spoke again, her eyes cast downward. "Well, maybe I did enjoy having him bring me my tea in the morning," she admitted sheepishly. With a wicked smile, Isaiah rose with a flourish and a deep bow to pour more tea for Miss Susannah. Everyone laughed at the young man's antics.

John suddenly grew serious. "You were on your way here, to see me? Why?" he asked Charles and Susannah.

"John, there is something that Susannah and I would like to discuss with you," Charles said soberly. "We've given this careful thought, and we have decided that we would like to go to the Oklahoma Territory with you to minister to the Indians there. Susannah and I can open a school as we did before, and you could help tend to The People's medical needs, just as Gray Hawk wanted. If you would like, you could live with us." He smiled at the joyful expression on John's face.

"We'd be a cord of three strands," John said with a laugh, "like Abraham read in the church this morning."

"Then, you agree?" Charles asked. John's shining eyes and bright smile were all the answer that Charles and Susannah required. Jumping to his feet, John came around the table to where the Thompsons were seated and threw his arms around the grinning pair.

In the dusky light of evening, Abraham sat back in his chair and surveyed the happy group. Miriam and Thomas, beloved newlyweds beginning the second part of their lives as conductors on the Underground Railroad; Charles, Susannah, and John, bound for the Oklahoma Territory to minister to the Cherokee Indians; and finally, Annie, Isaiah, and little Jacob, starting their brand-new lives, forever free of the iron shackles of slavery.

Three families, all different, but bound together as a single cord, Abraham mused, *and tied together by their dreams of freedom and equality for all.*

* * *

Leaving the groups to their own celebrations, Abraham quietly retired to his room, looking forward to a little reading and a lot of rest. Peering at himself in the mirror over the dresser, he rubbed his cheeks and chin with long, lean fingers. "Hmm," he muttered, eying his long, angled face. "Could Annie be right about the beard after all?"

Author's Notes

1838 was a turbulent year for the United States. Martin Van Buren was the new president, succeeding Andrew Jackson. The Act of Cherokee Removal was being enforced, resulting in the tragic "Trail of Tears." The Underground Railroad, which began in 1810 to help Africans escaping slavery in the south, was in full operation. The United States was in the throes of an economic depression, and John Wilkes Booth, future presidential assassin, was born.

By 1838, the Cherokee Indians of North Carolina and Georgia had adopted many of the customs of Europeans. They dressed like them, called their children common European names such as "John," and many converted to European religions. They designed roads and built schools. They had adopted a written alphabet developed by the famous Sequoyah. However, because of the discovery of gold in north Georgia, laws were passed that demanded the removal of the Indians to the Oklahoma Territory. The Cherokee were forced to travel on foot and by boat for hundreds of miles under terrible conditions. Because of the number of Indians who died during the ordeal, the journey was named the "Trail of Tears."

The Underground Railroad was well-established by 1838. Its many routes were used to transport hundreds of thousands of slaves to the North and Canada. In my research I discovered that houses, called "stations" on the Underground Railroad, were often painted black and white as a sign to fleeing slaves. Patterned quilts were used as signals. Wagons with false bottoms were useful for carry-ing the runaways, called "packages," but most slaves traveled to the North on foot under cover of darkness. Charles and Susannah Thompson, missionary teachers and "conductors" are fictional, but it is known that religious organizations, such as the Quakers, aided the slaves in their quest for freedom.

Many books have been written about Abraham Lincoln, the sixteenth president of the United States. We know that in 1838 Lincoln was a twenty-nine-year-old lawyer who worked for the circuit courts in Illinois. We also know that he was an excellent wrestler and swimmer, and that as a young man he had a vibrant sense of humor. Some historians refer to his superstitious nature and his interest in dream interpretation. I used the information that I gathered to create the young Abraham Lincoln you read about in these pages. His friends in this book, Miriam Hall and Thomas Richardson, are purely fictional, and there is no research that would lead us to believe that Lincoln had any involvement with the Un-derground Railroad. However, Lincoln is credited with these words, "Those who deny freedom to others deserve it not for themselves."

Lincoln actually did grow his famous beard at the suggestion of an eleven-year-old girl named Grace Bedell.

Traveling circuses were just becoming popular during this time period. The Flying Fishers Circus did not exist, but there was a family of trapeze artists named the Flying Fishers who performed for circuses. Although Annie and John's friend Dan was not real, his character was based on Dan Rice, a famous clown and animal trainer who lived from 1823–1900. He is credited with teaching a pig to tell time, and he taught an elephant to walk on a tightrope. Dan Rice and his famous red, white, and blue costume may have been the model for the famous "Uncle Sam" character that we know today. The real Dan Rice also became good friends with Abraham Lincoln later in life. The style of makeup worn by Annie and John to hide their skin color was made famous by another clown, Jo-seph Grimaldi, who lived in England from 1778 until 1837. There is no evidence that circuses were ever used by the Underground Railroad as a way to shuttle slaves to freedom.

The villain Willie Hall is based on the real-life criminal, John Murrell, who was born in 1804 in Mississippi. Murrell had the letters "HT" for horse thief branded on his thumb. He was convicted of Negro stealing, using a plan similar to the plot Willie uses to sell Isaiah. Murrell was also known as "Reverend Devil" because, like Willie, he preached during church services while his gang stole the horses tied outside the doors. John Murrell died in 1844.

I would like to thank Royce Collins and Don Moulder for their help in the development of the Gideon sticks. Your boundless daring was an asset to this book.

A apecial thank you goes to Teri Wilson for her constant support. Finally, I must thank Ben Brambrut's grandmother, my loyal friend and gentle critic, who dedicated hours of her time to the reading of this book.

Glossary

abolitionist—a person dedicated to ending slavery

athwart hawse—nautical term used to warn sailors that ships are about to collide

atsila—in Cherokee, "fire."

canku ota—in Cherokee, "many paths."

Cherokee Phoenix—newspaper started by Cherokee leader Sequoyah .

gathering sack—a pouch used by Native Americans to hold special items.

Gideon—an important leader in the Bible, his story can be found in the Old Testament book of Judges, chapters 6 through 8.

Hale, Sarah Josepha —author of "Mary Had a Little Lamb," written in 1830.

hihinalii—in Cherokee, "You are my friend."

hwilahl—in Cherokee, "Thou must go."

lions—Nineteenth-century Christians referred to temptations brought upon them by the devil as "lions."

nunnahi—in Cherokee, "a road of grief"

oracle—a fortune-teller, soothsayer.

packages—men, women, and children escaping from slavery on the Underground Railroad.

paste—a type of stone invented in the 1800s that was made from glass. Paste could be hand cut to create exact look-alikes of expensive jewels.

The Principal People—name for the Cherokee tribe.

Sequoyah—born in 1776, a great Cherokee leader who developed a system of writing for the Cherokee language.

shaman—Native American name for "healer."

tadeyastatkuhl—in Cherokee, "I will see you again."

About the Author

Holly Moulder taught elementary school in Newnan, Georgia, for more than twenty years. She spends her time writing and traveling to elementary and middle schools where she enjoys talking to students about her books, including *Eyes of the Calusa,* which won an honorable mention in the Writer's Digest Fifteenth International Book Competition. Mrs. Moulder lives in Coweta County, Georgia, with her husband Don (Mr. Leon), her daughter Lauren (Miss Grace), and former pirates Shelley and Shay Crittenden. She has one grand-dog named Leah—a Chihuahua, not a learned circus pig.

CPSIA information can be obtained
at www.ICGtesting.com
Printed in the USA
FFOW01n0020100415
12485FF